SAINTS PURGATORY MC

See Evil, Hear Evil, Become Evil, Purge Evil

SPIKE'S PERDITION

ANDI RHODES & LACY ROSE

To all of our loyal readers who took this crazy, wild ride with us… Thank you!
We couldn't have done it without all your support.

A NOTE FROM THE AUTHORS

The Saints Purgatory MC is a work of fiction. It is not a commentary on our thoughts or beliefs about religion. Spike's Perdition follows the club's Road Captain. He and Ivory have a rough road ahead of them, and you'll just have to read on to find out how they navigate it. Spike's story, like the others, is intended for adult readers. There are difficult topics which could be triggering for some.

If you would like more information regarding specific triggers, or if you'd like an idea of where the triggering topics occur so you can skip it, please feel free to reach out to either of us via email or social media. We're more than happy to discuss them further! And please note, if you do wish to skip those parts, it will not alter the story so much that you can't enjoy it.

Now, grab a jar of spicy pickles, peanut butter, some canned tuna, and a tall glass of chocolate milk, and brace yourself because this is gonna be one wild ride!

Much love,
    Andi and Lacy

SEVEN DEADLY SINS

Sloth
Pride
Lust
Greed
Gluttony
Wrath
Envy

Envy is the intense drive to possess something someone else has.

Envy is cured by kindness by putting the needs of others above the desire to be better than them.

PROLOGUE

SPIKE

Twenty-one years old...

"You 'bout done here, Hunter?"

I continue to turn the wrench I'm using to tighten the engine mount on the 1953 Indian Chief Roadmaster in front of me. My shift ended hours ago, but when I'm working on a bike, I tend to lose track of time. Lonnie Jacks, my mentor and owner of Jack's Restoration and Repair, tries to keep my enthusiasm reigned in, but in the eight years I've known him, he's rarely succeeded at that. If anything, he's fueled it.

"Gimme ten minutes."

"I swear, kid, you've gotta learn that life isn't all about work."

I've heard this same argument many times from him, but work is all I've got. Well, work and Lonnie.

"The bars ain't closin' anytime soon," I remind

him. "It ain't gonna kill ya to wait a little longer for your beer."

The familiar sound of a can being cracked open fills the shop. "Who said anything 'bout waiting?"

Shaking my head, I chuckle. "How the fuck is your liver still functioning, old man?"

"Good genes, I guess," he comments after gulping down a fair amount of Bud Light.

I wouldn't know anything about that. My genetic makeup is as much a mystery as the identity of Jack the Ripper. All I know is that the people who gave me life didn't care enough about me to quit whatever bullshit made them unfit to parent me.

"Hand me that rag, would ya?" I ask, nodding to the one I left sitting on the workbench.

And so it goes for the next twenty minutes. Lonnie drinks a few beers while I finish what I'm doing and clean up.

"Benny's gonna be really happy with the finished product," he says as we walk out of the shop and down the street toward the bar a few blocks away.

"I hope so."

Lonnie throws his arm around my shoulders, ignoring the spikes adorning my worn-out leather jacket. "Kid, you're the best motorcycle mechanic and restorer I know. Be proud of what you can do."

"I had a good teacher."

"Damn straight, you did."

Humble as always.

Lonnie caught me stealing a bag of chips at a local gas station when I was thirteen, and rather than turn me in, he followed me to the park where I'd made my camp and gave me an ultimatum: go with him to his shop and learn his trade or he'd call the cops.

I chose the former. It helped that it came with a warm bed in his spare room as well as food and clothing. I wasn't exactly thrilled when he made me enroll in school, but we compromised, and I finished my education online.

If it weren't for Lonnie, I'd either be dead or behind bars. I owe him everything.

"Would ya lookie there?" he says and whistles.

I follow his line of sight, and excitement buzzes through me at the line of Harleys parked in front of the bar. Based on the paint jobs and after-market parts, each one has had custom work done, and the closer we get, the more impressed I become.

"Recognize any of 'em?" I ask.

Lonnie shakes his head. "Not a one."

I make my way around each bike, taking in all the details, and when I reach the last one, something metallic in the front tire catches my eye. Kneeling down, I run my hands over the rubber and narrow my eyes when I recognize the shine as a nail head.

"Lonnie, run back to the shop and grab me a pair of pliers, would ya?"

While I wait for him to return, I try to work the nail out with my fingers, but progress eludes me. Heavy footsteps fall behind me, but I don't bother looking to see who it is, fully believing it's Lonnie.

"What the fuck do you think you're doin'?"

Before I can glance over my shoulder, large hands grip the back of my jacket and lift me enough to shove me back down to the pavement. I scramble to my feet so I can defend myself but freeze when I see a biker and several of his pals.

"I was trying to work a nail outta the tire," I say, raising my hands to show them I mean no harm.

One of the guys steps around me and squats near the front tire. When he glances over his shoulder, his face is hard as he communicates in sign language.

What the hell is he saying?

"How do I know you didn't put the nail there?"

I dart my eyes from one guy to the next, fear settling in my gut. I'm no slouch and can hold my own, but against these four, I wouldn't stand a chance.

Squaring my shoulder, feigning a confidence I don't feel, I level my gaze on the man who pushed me to the ground. "Because I'd never disrespect a bike like that."

"What do you know about bikes like this?" one of his friends asks.

Finally comfortable with where this interaction is headed, I relax slightly. "Everything."

"Everything?"

I nod.

"What year was the Harley Fat Boy introduced?"

"Nineteen ninety," I reply easily. He opens his mouth to speak, but I continue. "It was designed by Netz and Davidson and originally featured a Softail frame, shotgun exhaust, solid disc wheels, a 1340cc V twin engine, and a hand-laced leather seat." I take a deep breath. "Oh, and it was gunmetal gray with yellow trim."

"What year did Harley introduce the Chief?"

"They didn't. The Chief is an Indian motorcycle." I grin. "And it was introduced in 1922."

He glances to his friend on his left, a guy a bit older than him. "He's right, Soul," the guy says. "Dude knows his info."

Soul stares at me for a moment before relaxing his stance. "What's your name?"

"Hunter."

"Soul," he says, thrusting his hand out for me to shake. "These are my brothers, Grim, Frenzy, and Malice."

Before I can reply, movement catches my attention, and I look to see Lonnie walking toward us.

"Friend of yours?" Frenzy, the older guy, asks.

"Yeah," I confirm. "Lonnie Jacks. He owns—"

"Jack's Restoration and Repair," Frenzy says, with admiration. "Does some great work."

"Yes, sir, he does. Taught me everything I know."

"Everything okay here, Hunter?" Lonnie asks when he reaches us, a set of pliers gripped tightly in his hand.

I nod. "All good."

"I was just about to invite Hunter to have a beer with us," Soul says. "Care to join?"

Lonnie grins. "Sure."

"Lemme just get this nail out for ya real quick," I say, reaching for the pliers. "Then we can take the bike to the shop, and I'll patch up the hole before you head home."

"Don't worry 'bout it, man," Soul replies. "I'll have a prospect take care of it."

"A prospect?" I ask.

Two hours later, I'm three sheets to the wind and need carried back to the shop. The big guy, Grim, does the honors, treating me like a sack of potatoes. Lonnie fixes up the tire, free of charge since we didn't pay for a single drink.

"Here, man," Soul says, handing me a card.

"Gimme a call once your hangover wears off tomorrow. I think you'd make a great Saint, and if you're interested, we can talk prospecting more seriously."

I don't have time to formulate a response in my alcohol-addled brain before Lonnie and I are alone.

"C'mon, kid," he says. "You can pick up your bike tomorrow. I'm driving home."

As I follow him out to his 1957 Chevy Impala, my lips tilt into a smile.

You'd make a good Saint.

Soul is only the second person in my life to tell me I'd make a good anything.

CHAPTER ONE

IVORY

Present day…

"I DON'T THINK I CAN DO THIS."

The rumble of the turboprop engines vibrates through my body. The plane is filled with eight jumpers, but the one standing next to me is having a typical first-timer's reaction.

"You'll be fine." I squeeze her hand. "I promise, I'll be right there with you to signal when to pull the ripcord."

Kiera came in a couple of weeks ago with her entourage to celebrate her upcoming divorce. Her best friends convinced her that skydiving would be the perfect way to cleanse herself of her old life and jump into her new one. I, for one, wholeheartedly agree; however, I live for the adrenaline rush. From what her friends told me, Kiera is an introvert who prefers tranquil nights at home, curled up with a good book. I was shocked when she agreed to take the plunge.

Jenny, Kiera's best friend, slides up next to her. "Come on Kiera," she encourages. "I promise, you're going to feel so free."

I nod. "She's right. Plus, you can cuss the bastard all the way down."

Kiera chuckles before taking a deep breath. "Okay, I can do this."

"Damn right, you can."

"Five minutes out, Ivory," Milton, our pilot, announces over the speakers.

"Alright ladies, we're almost ready!" A chorus of 'Hell Yeah!' fills the air. "Remember, I'll point to you when it's your turn to jump." I adjust the GoPro camera on my helmet. I enjoy recording first-time jumpers because it's a great reminder for the customers of what they did and that they were brave enough to take that leap. "I'll be jumping with Kiera so I can get the footage you all want."

I quickly double-check everyone's harnesses, straps, and helmets. Then I pull my own harness as music fills the cabin. *Danger Zone* by Kenny Loggins is our signal that we're at the proper altitude to jump and we're clear to go.

"Here we go!" I yell and start pointing at Kiera's friends who give her a pat on the shoulder as they wait for their turn to jump.

Finally, it's our turn.

"I'm ready!" Kiera shouts over the music, her face no longer showing signs of doubt. Instead, her eyes narrow with determination, and her smile is contagious.

"Go!"

Kiera's screams fill the air when she jumps out. I count to three and follow her. Her head snaps up to look in my direction.

"Fuck you, Derek!" Kiera flips off the camera, and I chuckle.

I had a feeling that there was a little daredevil hiding inside of her, and I was right. I glance around quickly and see everyone else has pulled their cords and parachutes are littering the sky. I toss two fingers up in the air, signaling to Kiera that it's time to pull her rip cord. Kiera pulls her ripcord, and her body jerks as the parachute releases. I tug on my own cord, and we start the slower descent to the ground. Landings can be rough if you don't know what you are doing, but we aren't one of those mediocre companies that doesn't prepare clients. We give lessons and teach different methods of how to land without hurting yourself and absolutely will not take anyone up until they show they can follow our instructions and do things safely.

Kiera's friends rush her as she hits the ground. I land ten feet away and watch as they circle her, cheering and screaming simultaneously.

"That was fucking awesome!"

"We are *so* doing that again."

"This is definitely the best way to get over an ex."

I roll up my chute and walk over to the celebration. "How'd you like it, Kiera?"

"Best. Day. Ever!" she hollers. "Let's do it again."

I toss my head back and laugh. "Great, I created another adrenaline junkie."

A horn blares behind us, breaking up the group. I wave at Megan as she hops out of the *Chase the High* van. We built this business from the ground up and have a lot of activities for anyone looking for daredevil experiences.

"Did you ladies have a good time?" Megan asks as she starts helping me roll up the parachutes.

"Omigod, my heart is still pounding." Kiera bounces from foot to foot. "I had no idea what a thrill that'd be. What can we do next?"

"I think we corrupted her." I grin.

Megan gives her a thumbs up. "Welcome to the club."

After an hour of rolling up parachutes, we finally climb into the van and make our way back to headquarters. I close my eyes and bask in the joy of everyone retelling their experience of their first jump.

"Do you offer any other excursions?" Kiera asks.

I open my eyes and turn in my seat. "We have a wide range of activities if you're interested."

"Like what?" Jenny asks.

"We have rock climbing, hiking, skydiving, of cour—"

"Don't forget about our big white water rafting trip coming up," Megan adds.

Kiera's head snaps in Megan's direction "White water rafting?"

"Yep," I say, popping the 'p'. "Twice a year we take about ten to fifteen people with us to the Grand Canyon. We camp at night and battle the rapids of the Upper Colorado River during the day."

"In fact," Megan inserts. "We have a trip coming up in eight weeks. This'll be the last trip for the year out there."

"I could do that," Kiera claims.

Jenny rolls her eyes. "Girl, you hate camping. Remember the last time I tried to get you to go with me?"

"Derek said coyotes would get me. I was scared," Kiera mumbles, and everyone groans. "But I've gotten rid of the extra dead weight, and I know I can do it."

I smirk. "Fuck yeah, you can. Never let a man hold you back. You're strong, independent, and hella smart. You can do whatever you want."

"Do you have any more vacancies for the trip?" Jenny inquires.

I shrug. "I'll have to check the reservations once we get back, and I can let you know then."

"If you do, count me and Jenny in," Kiera says confidently. "No more holding back. I'm going to live my life."

"Thatta girl!"

We pull into the parking lot thirty minutes later and file into the office where our employee, Jeremy, is waiting.

"Who's ready to jump again?" he asks.

"We will definitely be signing up to do more." Kiera moves toward the desk. "Do you have any more room on the rafting trip?"

Jeremy's fingers pound away on the keyboard as he pulls up the reservation list. "We do. I have room for a couple more."

"Jeremy, go ahead and sign up Kiera and Jenny," I instruct.

Jeremy wags his brows. "Corrupted a couple more today, did ya?"

"You know it!" I hand Kiera and Jenny the itinerary and a packing list for the trip so they know what to expect and can be prepared. "This is all the information you should need, but feel free to call if you have any questions or concerns."

After everyone is stripped out of their jumpsuits and personal belongings are collected, they thank us again before heading out.

I throw myself into my chair and let out a huge sigh. "I'll never get over the rush I feel when I jump."

"Do you think they'll actually show up for the trip?" Megan sits across from me at her desk.

I nod. "Absolutely, the look on her face when she jumped said it all. It was like watching a literal weight being lifted off her."

"How about we grab the girls and go do something dangerous ourselves?"

"Like what?"

"Biker bar."

"Biker bar?" I ask, confused.

"Let's go to a biker bar tonight."

"You're kidding me, right?"

"Come on, you like living on the edge."

"True, but I also like the land of the living."

Megan laughs. "Nothing bad is going to happen.

"Obviously you've never read a book or watched a movie. Bikers have *danger* written all over them."

"Exactly… this is what we live for."

I stand. "Why not? I've already taken my life in my own hands today by jumping out of a plane. What's a couple of bikers?"

CHAPTER TWO

SPIKE

"I DON'T KNOW WHAT YOU WANT FROM ME."

I sneer at the man hanging from chains in the Confessional. He's not our typical victim because we, as a club, didn't seek him out for sins committed. But he's a sinner, nonetheless.

"I want you to admit what you did," I snap.

He points his toes in an effort to touch the floor and stop swaying, but he fails. I've got him strung up just high enough to give him false hope that he can somehow save himself.

"I was drunk," he insists.

Swinging as hard as I can, I hit him in the chest with the baseball bat. The sound of ribs cracking sends a tingle of satisfaction down my spine, although I'm surprised there are still ribs to break.

"Alcohol isn't an excuse for being a sexual predator."

"You won't get away with this," he says, his breath coming in short pants.

"Ah, see, that's where you're wrong. I can get away with anything. It's you who can't."

He opens his mouth to argue some more, but I'm sick of hearing his voice so I swing the bat one last time, connecting with his skull. His head lulls to the side as he sputters blood and takes his last breath.

"Go forth, sinners' souls, from this world. May you suffer in darkness, may your home be in Hell, and may the Devil fuck you with his horns."

The prayer we say after each purge brings me little comfort. The moment I saw this fucker walk into Purgatory last night, I knew he was gonna be trouble. I wasn't expecting him to try and force himself on a female customer in front of the entire bar, but he did. It amazes me that I can still be surprised by some human's behavior.

As I walk out of the Confessional and to the elevator, the adrenaline from the purge begins to wear off, and a weird sense of melancholy settles over me.

Things have changed since I patched into Saints Purgatory. My brothers seem to be falling like dominos and getting hitched while my life remains the same. Don't get me wrong, I wouldn't trade my life for anything, but I find that, lately, I crave some-thing… *more*.

When I reach the main level and the elevator door opens, I square my shoulders and make my way to the bar.

"Jacob, go clean up the Confessional," I order.

"What about the bar?" he asks. "I'm the only prospect here, and Soul put me on bartending duty."

I glance around the room until my eyes land on Frenzy's old lady. "Yo, Heather!"

She turns from her conversation with a few of the bunnies. "What's up?"

"Mind covering the bar while Jacob handles some club business?"

She smiles as she walks across the room and behind the bar. "Sure thing."

I return my attention to the prospect. "Get to cleanin'."

"You got it."

Jacob rushes to do my bidding, and as soon as Heather steps behind the bar, she gets me a beer. I carry it to my room so I can shower off the sinner's blood. As soon as I return to the main room, I get another beer and start making my rounds.

It doesn't take long to get tired of being social, and I find myself planting my ass on a bar stool, drinking more and more beer to dull my increasingly sour mood.

"Looks like you've got a fan."

I don't even look at Rogue as I roll my eyes and continue nursing whatever number beer is in my hand.

"If you're talking about Glitter," I say, referring to the newest club bunny. "She's not my type."

I may be tired and antisocial tonight, but I've seen Glitter staring at me in the mirror's reflection for at least the last half hour.

And she's exactly your type.

Rogue snorts. "Since when?" he asks as if reading my mind.

Giving up any hope of being left alone, I spin on my stool and glance around the room, pretending to look for someone. "Where's your better half?"

"Skye's at Purgatory," he says. "And even if she were here, she couldn't save you."

"Save me from what?"

Rogue grins. "Me, Glitter, yourself… Take your pick."

Downing the last of my beer, I groan. "Don't you have something better to do than give me a hard time?"

Rogue simply shakes his head and stalks away,

leaving me to marinate in my sour mood. I have no idea how much time passes or how much more alcohol I pour down my throat, but my head begins to spin.

"Hey, Spike."

I don't bother looking at Glitter as her voice swirls around me like the smoke from a bonfire in the Fall. She trails her nails down my arm, and my cock responds despite my brain's warning to ignore the sensation.

"Must have a lot on your mind tonight," she purrs. "It's not like you to get sloshed."

"Not 'loshed," I slur.

Glitter spins me around, and it takes all my willpower not to slide off the stool and crumble to the floor.

"Why don't you let me help you to your room and get you settled in?"

I command my head to shake, but it has a mind of its own, and I nod. "'Kay."

She slips her arm around my back and helps me to my feet. I'm a big guy, and most women wouldn't be able to hold my weight, but Glitter is tall and stronger than she looks.

When we reach my room, she grabs my hand and pushes it to the sensor that opens the door. The fact that I let her lead me around like a puppy dog is a testament to how drunk I am, but my dick doesn't seem to get the memo.

Traitor!

Glitter pushes me down on the bed, and then begins to strip. I'm vaguely aware of my clothes being removed from my body, and somehow, I manage to pull myself together enough to enjoy when she straddles my hips.

"Fuck, Spike," she moans. "You feel so damn good."

I thrust my hips in an effort to give her as much pleasure as I can, but I don't last long. Whiskey dick is a phrase that gets thrown around a lot, but I've never had that problem.

Thank fuck.

Glitter must get off because she quickly rolls to the side and curls against me. I don't know whether I pass out or fall asleep, but the next thing I know, my head pounds, and my mouth is bone dry.

I pull myself away from the woman next to me and glare at her. I have no memory of how I got to bed or why Glitter is here, but the lingering smell of sex gives me a sense of what happened.

"Get up," I demand, shaking her awake.

"Hmm?"

"Get the fuck outta my room."

"C'mon, Spike," she says sleepily. "I'm tired."

"Don't care," I snap.

She sits up and stares at me. "Are you really gonna kick me out after what we shared?"

I narrow my eyes. "What the fuck do you think?"

She holds my gaze for a moment before getting out of bed and grabbing her clothes off the floor. Glitter stomps to the door buck naked.

"You're an asshole," she bites out as she disappears into the hallway.

"Tell me something I don't know," I mumble.

CHAPTER THREE

IVORY

"Wow! It's packed in here."

Eric and I follow Megan as she pushes her way to the table Tia and Riley are occupying. She's not joking, it *is* crowded. We're lucky that our friends were able to come early and snag us a table. I slide my leather jacket off my shoulders and drape it on the back of my chair.

"You look sexy tonight."

I spin around to face Eric, flaring my black lace babydoll dress with a pink satin underlay that I paired with cowboy boots and wink.

"Thanks, hot stuff."

Eric and Megan are my besties, but all of us have been friends since high school, so we hang out a lot. Eric is a blast to go out with, and since he's trained in Krav Maga and boxing, he makes sure that men don't bother us unless we want them to. He's the big brother we both never had.

"Is it always like this?" Tia huffs as she tosses her purse onto the table.

"We've never been here," Riley sasses. "How are we supposed to know?"

Megan dragged us to Boulder City to hang out at Purgatory, a popular biker bar. The name alone gives me chills, but so far, it doesn't seem to be any different than the bars in Vegas.

"Take it down a notch, heifer." Eric laughs. "Just because you couldn't find a dick to hop on tonight, don't take it out on poor Tia."

"Fuck you, Eric," Riley says with no real heat behind her words. "I can't believe Owen blew me off."

"I think there's plenty of yummy standing in this bar for you to choose from." Eric licks his lips as his gaze lands on the tight ass of the man delivering drinks to the next table.

"Don't get us thrown out of here," I warn.

Eric grins. "I have no idea what you're talking about."

I smirk. "You know exactly what I'm talking about."

"Cock blocker," he pouts.

"Not every man you run into bats for your team."

"Anyone can be persuaded," he teases. "You just have to have finesse."

We all laugh as Mr. Tight Ass stops at our table.

"What can I get you tonight?" he asks.

"Your number and a round of tequila shots," Eric answers.

"And which pretty lady wants my number?"

Eric bats his eyes. "Me, handsome."

Mr. Tight Ass gulps. "Oh… um, well… I'm not…"

I hold up my hand to stop him before Eric can go in for the kill. "He's fucking with you."

"No, I'm not!" Eric argues. "I could bounce quarters off that ass."

"Eric!" I hiss and glance up at the guy. "Sorry about him. Contrary to popular belief, he really is housebroken. Unfortunately, sometimes when he's off his leash, he forgets."

Mr. Tight Ass laughs. "Wouldn't be the first time I've been hit on by a man. I'm flattered." He pauses and glances at Eric. "Sorry, dude, I don't swing that way."

Eric shrugs. "Your loss. Plenty of tall, dark, and dangerous to choose from here."

"Maybe." Mr. Tight Ass leans in between me and Eric. "I suggest Zach." He points out a man leaning against the bar with a cut that says Saints Purgatory MC on it.

Eric sighs. "Oooh, he's dreamy."

"I'll be right back with your shots," Mr. Tight Ass

promises. "I'm Tony, by the way. I'm supposed to be behind the bar, but the girls got slammed so I'm trying to help them get caught up. Can I get you guys anything else?"

"Bucket of long necks, please," I request.

"You got it, sweetness," he flirts. "I'll have Lana bring over your order when it's ready."

Megan's eyes roam around the club. "Damn, there's a lot of sexiness in here tonight."

"I've already tagged three contenders," Tia announces.

"Seriously?" I say exasperated. "Can we go out just once and not be on a man- finding mission?"

Eric bumps my shoulder. "Speak for yourself, babe."

"How long has it been?" Riley asks.

I dig my phone out of my purse, pretending to look at something. "How long has what been?"

Eric grabs my cell and tosses it to Megan. "How long has it been since you played hide the sausage?"

I toss my head back and laugh. "Hide the sausage? Really?"

"Come on, Ivory," Megan taunts. "There are plenty of bikers here to choose from."

I hold up my hand. "Bikers are fun to look at. Hell, sexy even, but they aren't relationship material. I live my life on the edge with our job, I don't need a dangerous man, panty-dropping or not, in my already chaotic life." I sigh. "I need stability. I've been burned way too many times. That doesn't mean I can't flirt a little, though."

"That's my girl!" Megan shouts.

"Hello, ladies," a deep sexy voice says from behind me. "Tony sent me over with your bucket of beer. Lana will be coming with those shots in a minute."

I swivel around on my chair and see Zach, the biker Tony pointed out. I take in his cut and see a patch with the word *Prospect* on the front. I have to admit, Zach is even better looking up close.

"Zach, is it?" Eric asks before I can say anything.

Zach smiles. "How'd ya know my name? Do I know you?"

"No." Eric shakes his head. "But I'd love to get to know you beneath the sheets. Tony said you'd be down to get dirty with me."

Zach's face turns a deep red. "I uh… no… I'm not… What the fuck?"

"I'll make you see stars, gorgeous," Eric whisper yells.

Everyone at our table bursts out laughing as Zach crosses his arms and stares down Eric.

"I don't know what you did to piss off Tony," I explain. "But he clearly set you up."

Zach glances around the table before his gaze lands back on Eric. "You don't want to fuck me?"

"Baby, if I thought for a minute you were into men, I'd throw you over my shoulder and find the closest broom closet to have my way with you," Eric states proudly. "Too bad for me, you like the snatch trap more."

"I'm gonna kill that fucker," Zach grumbles. "You make out with *one* waitress…"

"Oh, poor baby," I tease.

Zach throws his arm around my shoulders. "Wanna make it up to me?"

"Make it up to you?"

"Come dance with me."

I shake my head. "There's no music."

"There will b—"

"Ladies and gentlemen, please welcome Apple Caldwell," a man on the stage announces.

"Omigod!" we all shout in unison.

"No way, it can't be," Riley denies.

"I can't believe Apple is here!" Tia exclaims.

I tug Megan's hand. "Did you know Apple would be here?"

Megan's mouth hangs open. "I had no idea."

Apple saunters up to the microphone, and the crowd goes wild as music fills the air.

"How about that dance?" Zach asks.

"Go on," Megan encourages.

Tia nods. "Show him how it's done, Ivory."

I push back from the table and hop off the stool. "Why not?"

Zach leads me to the makeshift dance floor while Apple sings. He definitely has some moves as he pulls me close. Not to be outdone, I dip down as low as I can without flashing anyone the goods and slowly move up his body, shaking my ass as the bass flows through me.

"Shake that ass!" Eric yells.

"Fuck me," Zach moans as he grabs my hips and pulls me close. "Want to get out of here?"

I pat his chest. "Not tonight, Casanova, but thanks for the dance."

"Really?"

"Really," I state with finality. "I'm here with my besties celebrating the end of another successful week. This was fun though."

"Come on, how ca—"

"Zach!"

Zach's head snaps up when another man pushes his way through the throng of people. "What's up, Mark?"

Mark stares at Zach with his hands on his hips. "We're here as security for Apple, not to get your dick wet."

"Whoa," I say. "No one is getting their dick wet. Zach wanted a dance, and he got it. Now I'm gonna go and rejoin my friends."

"Sure, babe, whatever." Mark rolls his eyes. "Every woman in here wants to land a biker."

"Not this babe," I snap and spin on my heel to head back to my table. A hand reaches out and grabs my elbow, spinning me around. "You want to keep that hand, I suggest you let go of me."

"Let her go, Mark," Zach spits out. "It's my fault. I didn't think one dance would hurt anything."

A beautiful tattooed woman steps between us. "Is there a problem here?"

Zach bows his head. "No, Skye, we're good."

Skye narrows her eyes. "Then why are you manhandling my customers? Who, by the way, wasn't doing anything wrong by dancing with a prospect... like yourself, Mark."

"Look, I'm sorry. I was trying to get your attention to apologize. I didn't mean to offend you," Mark says sheepishly, barely looking into my eyes. "The crowd can get rowdy here, and we take Apple's security seriously. Zach is supposed to be helping, not flirting."

I hold up my hands. "No harm, no foul. You might want to work on your delivery though."

"Noted," Mark snickers and gestures to Zach. "Let's go, man."

"See ya around?" Zach asks hopefully.

I don't reply, but I give him a little wave.

Skye turns toward me. "I'm sorry about that."

"Not your fault."

"No, but I manage this bar, and Mark was out of line."

"Really, it's fine. I get why he was pissed. He obviously takes his security detail very seriously, which is good for Apple."

Skye grins. "That he does. Tell you what… Next round is on me."

"You don't have to do that."

"I want to. What'll you have?"

"Round of tequila shots."

"A girl after my own heart." Skye grins. "If I wasn't into totem poles…"

I snort. "Wow, and we've come full circle."

Skye blinks. "What'd I say?"

I pat her on the arm.

"It all started when Tony came to our table…"

CHAPTER FOUR

SPIKE

"MUST'VE BEEN SOME NIGHT."

It's been several days since my drunken state got me into trouble. Not that fucking a bunny is a bad thing, but Glitter has made sure to let everyone in the clubhouse know how big of an asshole I am. I guess it didn't help that she left my room naked, but that's on her.

I glare at Jez, Soul's twin. "Seriously? Even *you* heard about it?"

She grins and pats me on the arm. "I hear all, Spike. You should know that by now."

"If you're looking for your brother, you'll have to come back," I say with annoyance. "We're heading into church soon."

Her grin widens. "And that's why I'm here." I arch a brow, and she sighs. "Soul asked me to come."

If Prez is inviting Jez to join church, there must be something serious going on. Jez might be a hacker extraordinaire, and she does bring us a lot of *business*, but she's not a club member.

"Then I guess you might as well walk with me," I grumble.

"Whaddya think I was doing?" she quips.

When we reach the room where church is held, we both slip our cells into the box, but she keeps her laptop bag firmly on her shoulder.

"'Bout time you got here," Soul snaps when we enter, and the door slides closed behind us.

"It's her fault," I tell him.

"Don't blame her," Grim signs, his movements jerky. Then he smirks. "And that's fifty bucks."

"You can get it to me after church," Rogue, our treasurer, comments.

Jez drops her bag onto the table and lifts her hands. "Hell, even I know better than to not sign when the big man is in the room."

"Fuck off," I mutter.

"Ooooh," Jez taunts and looks to her brother. "That's another fifty, isn't it?"

"It is," Soul confirms.

Jez faces me and opens her mouth to continue taunting, but Malice stops her cold. "Sit the hell down, both of you. We've got shit to do."

"Yes, sir," Jez says.

Malice scrunches his nose and shakes his head. "No. Just… no."

Jez sighs. "Yeah, heard how weird it sounded the second it was outta my mouth. I'll leave all that to Apple."

"Speaking of Apple," Rogue says. "She keeps performing at Purgatory, and we'll all be able to retire early."

"Don't know about the rest of you, but I am definitely not ready for retirement of any kind," I tell them all. "The second you retire, life goes downhill."

"Maybe if you had someone to share your life with, you wouldn't feel that way," Thorn comments.

I turn my attention to Soul. "Don't we have club business to get to?"

Prez chuckles. "Yeah. I'm gonna turn things over to Jez because she brought this one to my attention."

Jez moves to the opposite end of the long table, quickly sets up her laptop, and connects it to the large screen so we can all see what she's seeing. When two images pop up, bile rises up the back of my throat, and white-hot rage threatens to turn my blood to lava.

"Jesus," Possum mutters. "A little warning next time."

The pictures are of two children, both no older than three or four, and both lying in hospital beds with casts and severe bruises. I don't know who did this to them, but if I know Jez, we're about to find out.

"Sorry," Jez comments, fury in her tone. "But it only gets worse from here."

"Who the fuck did this to them?" Malice demands.

"Oh, please tell me I can gut the motherfucker," Grim signs.

"We're all gonna get a turn," Soul snaps. "Now, let her finish."

All eyes turn to Jez expectantly. She's staring at the images on the screen, a pained look on her face. As members of Saints Purgatory MC, we see the worst of the worst, and Jez has become an integral part of what we do. But we're still human, and some things affect us more than others.

Like kids who've barely survived a monster... Kids like I was.

"Carter Maxwell is the piece of shit who did this," Jez says, her voice monotone. "Fortunately, he was arrested. Unfortunately, that makes it harder for us to purge him."

"Us?" Grim signs, eyebrow arched.

"You know what I mean," she replies dismissively.

"How does shit like this even happen?" Fort, our techie, asks.

"It happens more than you think," I snap.

"He's right," Soul agrees. "And when we're done with Mr. Maxwell, there'll be one less embodiment of evil on this Earth."

"But he's in…"

My mind spirals back in time as my brothers try to come up with a plan to get the scumbag out of jail to be purged.

"I wanna go home."

The social worker looks at me with annoyance and shakes her head. "I'm sorry, Hunter, but you can't go home."

She's just one in a long line of social workers who've taken me away from my parents. You'd think I'd be used to it by now, but I hate foster homes.

I glance at the cast on my arm and will my mind to ignore the pain. "I won't stay with another stupid family."

"You don't ha—"

"Spike, you with us?"

I shake my head to clear it and level my gaze on Soul. "Yeah, Prez."

"How long do you need?" he asks.

"Uh…"

Soul narrows his eyes, his disappointment show-ing. "We need a route to Wichita, Kansas so we can scope out the jail and see if a breakout is a viable option."

"Right." I nod. "I can have that in less than an hour."

"Get it to me tomorrow morning," Prez instructs.

"You got it."

Church lasts another fifteen minutes, and then we all disperse. I make my way to my room to quickly come up with a game plan for whoever is going on the Wichita run. It takes some doing to avoid other MC territories, but in the end, I get it done in forty-five minutes.

After delivering it to Soul, I decide to head to Purgatory. The reminder of my childhood and the now burned-in-my-brain images have put me in a funk that only alcohol and pussy can cure.

And I'm not in the mood for familiar pussy.

CHAPTER FIVE

IVORY

"YOU HEIFERS ARE NEVER GONNA BELIEVE WHAT I JUST found out."

My head snaps up from the financial reports I've been going over for the past hour as Eric barrels into our office.

Megan gasps, clutching her chest. "What the hell, Eric? You can't just run in here, scaring the shit out of us."

"Bitch, please." Eric waves off her dramatics. "We have places to go."

I smirk. "And where exactly are we going?"

Megan and Eric share a knowing look before Megan grabs her purse from inside her desk. "Come on, Ivory. We have to go get ready. Tia is meeting us there."

I cross my arms. "Again, where are we going and get ready for what?"

"Purgatory," Eric replies.

I shake my head. "Uh, nope."

"Come on, Ivory," Megan begs. "We had a blast last time."

"We had a blast?" I question. "Was that before or after I was manhandled by a biker?"

Eric rolls his eyes. "Dramatic much?"

"I have no desire to *ever* go back to that bar."

"Apple's gonna be there again," Eric states matter-of-factly.

"How do you know that?"

Eric smiles. "Tony told me when I was cashing out our bill."

"Why didn't you tell us?"

Eric shrugs. "Slipped my mind I guess."

"Bullshit," Megan laughs. "You knew you could use this as leverage to get Ivory to go back there."

"Possibly." Eric winks. "Question is, did it work?"

"I wonder why Apple keeps going back to Purgatory," I mumble.

Megan stands from her desk. "Who cares? She's gonna be there tonight, and I'd rather pay a cover charge to get in than try to get tickets to a sold-out concert."

"Fine," I mutter as I grab my purse and hurry to follow them out. "I need to go home and get ready."

"What the hell have I been saying?" Eric asks exasperated.

I giggle. "Now, who's being dramatic, Queenie?"

"Damn straight, and don't you forget it." Eric swats my ass as we lock up. "Move it, woman. We're already behind schedule."

A couple hours later we're seated at a high-top table in the middle of Purgatory. I'm glad we arrived early because people are piling in, and there are a lot more bikers wearing Saints Purgatory cuts.

Damn, these men are F.I.N.E.

They must really like the beer here. I find it hard to believe that they're fans of Apple.

"Where's Riley tonight?" Tia asks, interrupting my thoughts.

Megan snickers. "To quote Eric, she's playing 'hide the sausage' with Owen."

"You came back," Zach says, appearing out of nowhere. His eyes roam over my body. "Holy fuck, you look sexy as hell."

"This old thing?" I gesture to my outfit. "Just something I had lying around my house."

Tonight, I'm wearing a strapless blush pink sequined mini dress with black stilettos. I wanted to wear jeans and a t-shirt, not wanting to draw attention to myself again from any biker, but Eric dared me.

And I never back down from a dare.

"I'd ask if you want to dance, but I'm on crowd control tonight," Zach whines. "I can find you after Apple's done, though."

Sure, he's good-looking, but I didn't feel any sparks between us when we danced the other night.

"That's sweet, Zach," I say with a smile, not wanting to hurt his feelings. "I have to be honest, I'm not looking for a rel—"

"Don't sweat it," Zach interrupts. "Save me a dance though?"

"I'm not sure how late we're staying, but sure, if we're still here."

Zach winks. "Until then."

"He's nice," Tia comments. "You should hook up with him."

"Hi again," Skye greets as she saunters up to our table. "Hook up with who?"

"Zach," Eric replies. "Ivory doesn't do bikers, apparently."

I shake my head. "It's not that. They have bad decisions written all over them."

"Yeah, they do," Skye agrees. "And I'd make that bad decision a million times over again."

"Wait... what?" I ask, confused.

"Do you see the tall, sexy man with the glasses, giving off Clark Kent vibes but in a bad-boy Lex

Luthor kinda way?" Skye gestures over to the bar. We all crane our necks to see over the crowd and nod. "That's my old man, Rogue. He's part of Saints Purgatory MC. In fact, the club owns this bar."

"I thought *you* owned the bar."

Skye shakes her head. "I'm the manager, but the club owns the place."

"That makes sense," Megan admits. "It *is* a biker bar, after all."

"Okay, that does make sense, now that you mention it," I agree. "Why does Apple perform here so much?"

"Apple is married to Malice, Vice President of the club." Skye points to a man scowling by the stage. He's definitely giving *fuck around and find-out* vibes.

"No way," Eric argues. "He's got the whole pissed-off *Jared Leto* thing going on."

"That he does, but it's true," Skye says with a chuckle. "What can I get you all tonight? Tequila shots?"

"Yes, and some whiskey sours for all of us, please," I say.

"How about some fried pickles and nachos?" Megan asks.

"You know that goes right to my thighs!" Eric yells.

"You'll just have to find a man to work off the

extra calories then," I snicker. "Some of us need our carbs."

"Coming right up!" Skye says cheerfully. "Good to see you all again. Enjoy the show."

"Damn, the eye candy in here tonight is *ahhmazing*," Eric drawls.

Megan bobs her brows. "Agreed."

"How about we make this interesting?" Tia speaks up.

Fuck… this is going to end badly. I can feel it.

"What'd ya have in mind?" Eric asks.

Tia is about to respond, but a waitress arrives with our drinks and tells us that our food will be out soon.

As soon as she walks away, Tia rubs her hands together, and a sinister smile forms on her face. "Megan, I dare you to blow a kiss and wave to that biker walking this way."

"I thought you said we're gonna make this interesting." Megan quips before tossing back her shot.

Megan flutters her lashes while raising her arm. She puckers her lips, presses her hand to them, and blows dramatically at the man walking by. She finishes her task by wiggling her fingers at him.

The man skips a step but then straightens, making a beeline right for us.

"You summoned me, gorgeous?" he asks, stepping up to our table. His patch reads *Possum*.

Megan grins. "Possum? I think there's a story there."

"Wouldn't you like to know?" Possum leans in. "Come dance with me, and I'll tell you all about it."

"You're on." Megan hops down from her stool and takes his hand as he leads her to the dance floor.

Apple takes the stage, and pandemonium breaks out, but it quickly eases when she begins to sing.

"Alright, Eric. It's your turn," Tia announces.

"Bring it on shorty," he taunts.

I glance around the bar and see a beautiful man walking toward us with a tray of food. He's wearing a red off-the-shoulder top with black glitter writing that says 'I don't bite, I suck'. As he gets closer, I notice he's wearing black leather pants and matching high-heeled boots.

"See that guy heading right for us?" I ask, and Eric smirks. "Call him 'Daddy' and get his number."

"I thought you'd give me a hard one," Eric whispers.

"Here you go!" the man announces as he places the food on the table. "Can I get you all anything else?"

"Just your number, Daddy," Eric purrs while tracing his fingers up the guy's arm.

"Daddy, huh? I like that." He pulls Eric off his chair before weaving his fingers through his hair and pulling his face closer. "Most people call me RaRa, but you can call me *Daddy* anytime."

RaRa crashes his lips to Eric's, and I swear they both groan. For a moment, I feel like I need to give them privacy, but then RaRa breaks the kiss.

"Wow," Eric mumbles, his eyes glazed over.

"My thoughts exactly, handsome." RaRa holds out his hand. "Give me your phone."

Eric hands him his phone, and RaRa puts in his number. After returning it to Eric, he pulls his own out of his back pocket and shows Eric the screen. "Now I have your number, too. I have to get back to work. Don't be a stranger."

RaRa sashays away as Eric watches his retreating back. "Did that just happen?"

"Yes, yes it did," I answer since Tia's mouth is frozen open.

"Fuck, that was hot!" Eric exclaims. "Should I call him? That man gave me chills."

"Hell yeah, you should call him," I encourage. "I think you both broke Tia."

Tia blinks rapidly. "I'm fine... shocked, but fine. I can't believe that just happened."

"Believe it, babe," Eric brags. "I'm a stud."

"That you are, Queenie," I confirm.

"Dear lord, that man can dance," Megan announces as she takes her seat. "Did I see Eric kissing someone?"

"You looked like you were having fun," I reply.

"That was RaRa. He delivered our food, Eric called him *Daddy*, and they exchanged numbers after swapping spit," Tia explains.

"I take it that was Eric's dare?" Megan asks.

I nod. "Yep."

"Okay, Tia. It's your turn." Megan taps her fingers on the table as she glances around the bar.

"I got one," Eric shouts. "Tia, you have to go twerk on the dance floor."

Tia gets up and walks to the middle of the bar while Apple switches to a slower song. That doesn't stop her though. She places her hands on her knees and starts jiggling her ass, garnering more than a few passing stares.

We all howl with laughter as she makes her way back to us.

"Okay, your turn, Ivory," Tia singsongs as she sits down.

"I'm gonna sit this one out guys," I decline.

"You can't!" Tia pouts. "We've all done one."

I shrug. "I'm not in the mood tonight. Can't we just sit here and enjoy the rest of the show?"

"You've never backed down from a dare, Ivory," Eric taunts, parroting my earlier thought.

He's right. Besides, every dare so far has been tame compared to some of the

situations we've found ourselves in before.

I take a sip of my drink. "Fine, let's see what you got."

CHAPTER SIX

SPIKE

"Better watch it, or you're gonna turn into a creeper."

I glance over my shoulder at Skye who's wiping down the bar even though she and the other bartenders at Purgatory keep it relatively spotless. I've been here for hours, scoping out my options, but the last thirty minutes I've been focused on the group in the corner. More specifically, the chick in the shiny mini-dress and stilettos.

"Don't know what you're talking about," I mutter before downing the rest of my beer.

"Why don't you go over and introduce yourself?" she suggests as she gets me another beer.

The girl throws her head back and laughs at something, and her smile practically lights up the smoky bar. My cock stirs behind my zipper, and I don't even bother to hide having to adjust myself.

"Maybe I will," I reply, no longer trying to deny that I'm interested.

"Go get 'er, Spike," Skye calls while I start to walk toward the group.

Apple's song comes to an end, and the closer I get to them, the more I can hear their conversation, and the more intrigued I become.

"Okay, your turn, Ivory," the girl who was just twerking singsongs as she sits down.

Finally, a name to go with the face.

"I'm gonna sit this one out guys," Ivory declines.

"You can't! We've all done one."

She shrugs. "I'm not in the mood tonight. Can't we just sit here and enjoy the rest of the show?"

"You've never backed down from a dare, Ivory," the only guy in the group taunts.

She seems to think about what to do before taking a sip of her drink and declaring, "Fine, let's see what you got."

Twerking girl scans the bar and grins widely when her eyes settle on Malice, who's standing near the stage so he can be close to Apple.

"I've got just the dare for you," she says.

"Aw, fuck, Tia," Ivory groans. "Get that look off your face. You know how I feel about bikers."

Hmmm... This should be interesting.

"I do," Tia confirms. "But you said you wanted to see what we had, so…"

"I double dog dare you to take a chance on a biker."

The words are out of my mouth as soon as I'm within earshot of the group, and all eyes turn to me.

"Excuse me?" Ivory says, her gaze traveling from my face down to my boots and back again. "Were you eavesdropping?"

The guy smacks her playfully on the shoulder. "Who the fuck cares, heifer?"

My hackles rise at the nickname, and I step closer to him. "Call her that again, and we're gonna have a real fuckin' problem."

Ivory settles her hand on my bicep, and I swear sparks fly between us. "He didn't mean anything by it." She turns to her friend. "Did you, Eric?"

"Of course not," Eric says. "Hell, Ivory's my bestie. I'd never do anything to hurt her."

I relax slightly. "Good to know."

"Now that that's settled," Tia begins. "Let's get back to that whole double dog dare thing."

I grin, my eyes remaining on Ivory. "Seems to me that you were up in your little game. Figured I'd help with that."

"I don't date bikers," Ivory quips, crossing her arms over her chest.

Clearly, she doesn't realize how much that little movement pushes up her cleavage, and I sure as hell ain't tellin' her.

"Gonna have to dance with me first, sweetheart," I say. "Then maybe I'll consider dating."

"Ooh, I like him," Eric beams. "Can we keep him, Ivory? Please?"

"I dare you to dance with…" Tia glances at me and drops her gaze to my patch. "Spike."

"Hunter," I supply. "My name is Hunter. My road name is Spike. You can call me either."

Tia smiles and faces Ivory. "I dare you to dance with Hunter slash Spike."

Ivory rolls her eyes. "You sure? You don't want to think about it for a minute, maybe come up with something… better?"

"Oh, she's sure," Eric states.

"Fine."

Ivory grabs my hand and tries to drag me to the middle of the bar, but I don't budge. When she glares at me over her shoulder, I arch a brow.

"It'd be nice if you didn't act like you were on your way to be slaughtered," I tease.

"For all I know, I could be."

"I think I can do a little better than that. Be right back."

Tugging out of her grip, I hurry toward the stage and Malice.

"She's hot, bro," he says when I reach him.

"And I need her hot for me," I counter. "Get your old lady to play that song."

"What song? She's got a lot of them."

"You know the one…" I snap my fingers as I try to remember the name. "Drives women crazy and ma—

"I got ya covered." Malice pats me on the shoulder before shoving me back in the direction I came from.

Ivory remains where I left her, her stare seeming to penetrate clear through to my soul. The intensity of it sends my heart rate through the roof, and I take several deep breaths to calm myself. She's already wary of bikers and jumping her bones right here, right now won't win me any brownie points.

When I reach her, Apple shifts to a new song, and Ivory's eyes light up.

"I love this song!" she exclaims when I reach her.

"Soul of a Saint," I say, the title coming to me out of nowhere. "Everybody loves it."

"Did you do this?" she asks.

"What?"

"Did you get her to play this?"

I grin. "Yep."

"Hmm."

Grabbing her hand, I pull her close and wrap my arms around her as the song's beat fills the room. For a moment, Ivory stiffens, but she quickly relaxes against me.

I don't know how long we dance, but when she shifts back and levels her gaze on mine, I know one thing for certain: I'm getting laid tonight.

Thank you, Apple.

Ivory looks over her shoulder at her friends and some silent conversation must take place because the next thing I know, they're waving and she's leading me toward the door.

"Where ya taking me?" I ask, not really giving a damn.

She stops before exiting and spins to face me. "You double dog dared me to take a chance on a biker, did you not?"

"I did."

"Were you really just looking for a dance? Or did you have more in mind?"

"Depends."

"On?"

"I might be a biker, but contrary to what you seem to think, we're not all bad. I'd never want you to do something you didn't want."

"But you do want more than a dance?" she asks again.

I smirk and lower my eyes to my very obvious erection. "What do you think?"

"I think we need to get outta here."

Twenty minutes and an Uber ride later, and we're checking into a motel near the interstate. I know next to nothing about this chick, so the clubhouse was out, and she said she lives about an hour away, and I wasn't waiting that long to get her naked.

"So…" Ivory dips her chin. "We're really doing this."

I close and lock the door to our room before spinning her around to pin her against the wall. "Only if you want to."

Please want to.

She hesitates for a moment, and just when I'm about to step back, she jumps up and wraps her legs around my hips. I slam my lips against hers and dart my tongue past the seam to swirl around the recesses of her mouth.

Ivory moans, and I swallow the sound. Without breaking the kiss, I carry her to the bed and sit on the edge of the mattress with her on my lap. Her dress is hiked up, exposing her thighs, and I run my hands up her flesh until I reach her ass.

"Mmm, thong," I groan. "I approve."

"Good to know."

I rear back and grin. "That's the kinda statement that makes me think there'll be an encore."

"Let's see if you can get a standing ovation first."

Growling, I stand and twist, tossing her onto the bed. She laughs, and the husky sound goes straight to my dick. I slowly take off my cut and hang it over the back of one of two chairs in the room. Then I strip out of my clothes, letting them fall into a pile on the floor.

"Holy shit," Ivory mutters, her eyes widening as she takes in my hard cock.

I take myself in hand and tug. "I'll fit."

She scoots into a sitting position and shakes her head. "I'm not so sure about that."

"Get that dress off so we can find out," I command.

She wastes no time yanking it over her head. My eyes are immediately drawn to her lace bra as she reaches behind to unhook it. Ivory slowly drags the straps down her shoulders, letting it fall to reveal her breasts. I stroke my cock while I admire her perfectly curved body. With her gaze on my dick, she cups her breasts, squeezing and pulling at her nipples.

I come undone at the sight. Pushing her down gently, I crawl over her body. She slips her hands around my neck and pulls me in for another kiss. She tastes like wintergreen and booze, and the combination is intoxicating.

As my tongue glides across her lips, she drags her feet up the back of my legs. When she pulls away again, she levels her eyes on mine.

"So, biker boy," she purrs. "Ya gonna show me what ya got and make this double dog dare worthy, or are we just gonna make out like teenagers?"

My eyebrows shoot up, and I grin. "Be careful what you ask for," I say, and then I reach between us to line my cock up with her entrance.

Ivory moans loudly, and I thrust inside her, eliciting a more guttural response. I lean close to her ear and brush my tongue around the shell.

"Told ya I'd fit," I whisper, and she shivers.

I piston in and out, in and out, the walls of her pussy practically vibrating around me. Ivory digs her heels into my lower back and her nails into my shoulder blades. She lifts her hips to meet each of my thrusts, and every one of my nerve endings seem to burn from the sparks flying between us.

I've had my fair share of sex, but with Ivory, it's primal. It's explosive. It's… perfect.

Sliding my hand down, I flick her clit with my thumb, and she bucks wildly.

"Aw, damn," she groans, throwing her head back.

"Come for me," I order, pinching her clit as I continue hammering into her cunt.

Her entire body quivers, and she flies over the edge of ecstasy. My balls draw up tight, and my spine tingles just before I explode. Our orgasms seem to last forever, in the best possible way, and when we each settle, I roll off her.

"That was—"

"Double dog dare worthy," I state.

Ivory laughs. "It was." She curls into my side. "But please tell me that's not all ya got?"

I turn my head to look at her, and the gleam in her eyes has my dick swelling again.

"We've only just begun."

CHAPTER SEVEN
IVORY

"Hmmm."

Clutching my stilettos to my chest, I hold my breath while Spike rolls over on the bed. I slowly exhale as I lower my arms, quietly unlock the door and slip out, leaving behind the sexier-than-sin biker who's still naked under the covers.

Blowing the hair out of my face, I slip my shoes on in the hallway and quickly exit the motel. I pull up the Uber app on my phone and book a ride. As soon as I'm back to my own vehicle, I unlock the driver's door and slide in, resting my head on the steering wheel and willing my heart to stop pounding.

Coward!

I left him behind with no explanation. It was a dare, a one-time fling. We didn't make promises. We both knew the score.

He won't be mad, will he?

Shaking my head to rid the intrusive thoughts, I put the key in the ignition. On the drive home, my mind drifts back to our incredible night together. I lost count of how many orgasms I had because Spike is definitely a giver.

After pulling into my driveway, I throw the car into park and exit on autopilot. Unlocking the front door, I step over the threshold with my head in the clouds. I don't even remember how I got home, which is crazy because in my line of work, paying attention to one's surroundings is a must. Too many accidents happen when someone isn't fully aware of the world around them. That explains how I missed Megan's car parked in the street.

"Where've you been?" Megan screeches.

I toss my keys and purse onto my entry table. "You were at the bar," I remind her. "You know where I was."

"Have you checked your phone?"

Now that she mentions it, no, I haven't. Did I leave it at the motel?

Panicking, I empty my purse. My phone clatters to the floor. I scoop it up and notice the thirty-four missed calls and countless text messages.

"Sorry," I mumble. "I don't know how I missed all these."

Megan pulls me into the living room and down onto the couch.

"What happened?" she asks. "I honestly thought you guys would fool around in an alley or something, but you never came back. When we paid our tab and went outside, your car was there, but you were gone."

"Sorry. I was planning to be back by last call. I swear."

Megan smirks. "I take it from your appearance that you got a good dickin',"

I sigh. "You have no idea."

I didn't have time to wash my face before I made my escape. I have raccoon eyes from mascara and eyeliner, smeared lipstick surrounds my mouth, and I haphazardly threw on my clothes. The wrinkles in my dress could tell stories.

"Spill. Now."

"We got outside the bar and realized we had no real place to go. I'm adventurous, but not enough to be caught naked in my car banging a local biker." I fidget with my dress. "Spike recommended a motel that was nearby, and we caught an Uber. Next thing I know, it's morning, and I ducked out and hid my shame all the way back to my car."

"Wait, you went to a motel and didn't shower before you left?" she asks incredulously.

"I was in a hurry to get home."

"Uh-huh, for what?"

"What do you mean, for what?"

Megan smirks. "Well, it certainly wasn't to check on your friends you abandoned last night, or you would've checked your phone and called one of us back."

"How did you get home?" I ask, remembering I was their ride, and I had my keys with me.

"RaRa offered us a ride. He and Eric were all over each other last night after you left." She flips her hair over her shoulder. "Now, why were you in such a hurry to get home? Was Spike a dick this morning or something?"

I shift uncomfortably. "Not exactly."

"You're being very evasive."

"Ugh." I cover my face with my hands. Megan pulls them away and stares into my eyes, concern marring her face. "It's not like that. I think I might've done the wrong thing... but we agreed. It's not like he di—"

Megan holds her hands up. "Whoa, back up a minute. What are you talking about? What did you do?"

I jump to my feet and pace back and forth in front of the couch. "I left."

"Obviously, you're standing right here."

"You don't understand," I say with a shake of my head. "I left him in the bed. I snuck out like a thief in the night… or morning."

"Hold on." Megan reaches out and grasps my wrist. I halt my steps as she pulls me back down. "Let me get this straight. You did the horizontal tango with Mr. Sexy-as-fuck Biker, spent the night with him, and left without saying 'thanks for the orgasms'? Or was he so terrible in bed you didn't want to face him?"

"Nothing like that." I toss a pillow at her. "That was probably the best sex I've ever had."

"Then what gives with the disappearing act?"

"It was a dare. A one-night stand."

"So, that means you couldn't say goodbye?"

"No strings attached… no commitment. We agreed."

"And yet you sit here, worried about doing something wrong by sneaking away?" Megan asks. "Help me understand. Do you like him?"

Do I like him?

No. No way could I have feelings for someone after one night of mind-blowing orgasms. I don't even know him.

"It was sex, a release."

"You're avoiding my question," Megan teases.

"No, I don't even know him," I protest.

"But you'd like to," Megan counters.

I sigh. "It doesn't matter. Nothing will ever come of it. Sure, the sex was amazing, but that doesn't mean we're destined to be together."

"It could, though."

I shake my head in denial. "No, Megan, it couldn't. He's a biker, for fuck's sake."

"What does that have to do with anything?"

"Bikers are not monogamous. They cheat. They're not faithful. I can't be with someone like that. I need stability."

"I didn't get that vibe from the other bikers there. They really seemed enamored with their woman."

"Spike overheard a conversation between all of us and dared me. He has Playboy written all over him. No one can be that good in bed and not have tons of women he's practiced on."

"That's not fair, Ivory," Megan protests. "You should give him a chance if he wants one. It's not like you were a virgin before jumping into bed with him."

I'll never admit it because she's right. I've had my share of sexual partners, but never a one-night stand. Spike seemed at ease with a complete stranger, while the whole time I was freaking out.

Liar! You were egging him on, really getting into the

whole dare aspect of it all. And definitely not during the orgasms. And you felt safe enough to fall asleep with him.

"We'll never know because I'm *never* going back to Purgatory," I say with finality.

Megan sighs in frustration. "If that's what you want, I'll back you. What'll you do if he comes searching for you?"

"That's easy… I never gave him any indication I wanted to see him again or any way for him to find me," I say matter-of-factly. "The only way he'll find me is if I step foot in Boulder City again. Now that I know that's the home of Saints Purgatory, the hounds of hell couldn't drag me back there."

"Famous last words."

"Please, he was amazing in bed, but having an amazing cock doesn't mean he's worth the trouble of pursuing."

"Alright. How about we work out the details for the whitewater rafting trip?" Megan asks, changing the subject. "That'll be here before we know it."

I'm right about this. Nothing but pain and heartache can come from dating a biker.

Yeah, keep telling yourself that.

CHAPTER EIGHT

SPIKE

"Well, well, well, look what the cat dragged in."

I toss my keys at Skye, who dodges them and leans against the couch as I walk from the elevator to the bar. Despite being thoroughly fucked, I'm in a shit mood and don't need anyone's crap on top of it.

"Did you just throw your keys at her?" Rogue demands as he grabs the back of my cut, bringing me to a halt.

"Calm down," Skye says sweetly. "I was giving him a hard time."

"I don't give a flying fuck if you called him cage-driving ogre or spit in his Cheerios," Rogue snaps.

"Relax, bro," I cajole, which only results in his grip getting tighter. "I wasn't trying to hurt her."

He shoves me. "Do it again, and we'll have a real problem."

"Got it."

I continue across the room, grateful to have

dodged that bullet, but my relief is short-lived when Skye catches up to me and threads her arms through mine.

"So, things didn't go well?" she asks.

"What are you talking about?" I counter.

She smacks me playfully. "Oh, come on. I saw you leave with Ivory last night."

I halt and stare at her. "You know Ivory?"

She shrugs. "Well, not really. She and her friends have come into Purgatory a few times, and I managed to get her name."

"Oh."

"Oh?" she parrots. "That's it?"

"What do you want from me?" I snap. "We fucked. It was great. She was gone when I woke up. End. Of. Story."

"Oh, damn," Malice says as he joins us. "What'd ya do to deserve that?"

"Nothing," I bark.

At least, nothing that I know of.

"Maybe she had to be somewhere," Skye suggests.

"Maybe." The thought hadn't crossed my mind, honestly. But it does make me feel a little better about being left. "Doesn't matter. I got what I needed from her."

"From who?" Glitter asks as she strolls toward us.

70

Goddammit! How many people are gonna see their way right into this conversation?

"Some chick he slept with last night," Rogue offers.

Glitter visibly stiffens, but she quickly forces her shoulders to relax and smiles. "Sucks to be you. Maybe you should stick to us bunnies? None of us would leave you hangin'."

"She didn't leave me hanging," I bite out. "Not in the way you mean, anyway."

"But she left," Glitter states. "That's just as bad, isn't it?"

Normally, no. But for some reason, with Ivory, it bothers the ever-loving piss outta me. I turn away from Glitter, effectively cutting her out of the conversation.

"Asshole," she mutters loud enough for me to care.

"Get lost," Rogue barks at her, and the clickity-clack of her heels as she exits the common room follows.

"I'm gonna go shower," I announce.

"Wait a second," Skye demands. "Are you really that upset that Ivory left this morning?"

I hesitate and think about how to answer her question without triggering a million more. "More annoyed than anything."

"Right," Rogue taunts. "And it's annoyance that has you looking like you swallowed a fucking lemon. You're pissed, bro. Just admit it."

"I'm not pissed," I insist. "I'm…"

"Hurt," Skye suggests quietly.

Scoffing, I shake my head. "Definitely not."

"C'mon, babe," Rogue begins. "Spike's a certified bachelor. He's not gonna get butt-hurt because some chick doesn't stay for breakfast."

"I'm out," I state and quickly move away from the two of them before I get caught in between an argument. There's no denying that they love each other, but Rogue doesn't always think before he speaks.

"Hey, where ya been?" Soul asks when I pass him in the hall.

I groan. "Jesus, can't a guy stay out all night without needing permission?"

Prez holds his hands up. "Whoa, chill."

I thrust my hand through my hair. "Sorry."

"You okay, man?"

"Fine. Just hungover."

That's not a total lie. I did drink a lot last night and have the headache to prove it.

"Well, go shower off the grunge and meet me in the meeting room. I wanna go over the route you planned."

"You got it."

Soul continues toward the common room while I go to my room. As I shower off my frustration, my mind flashes back to the many times I made Ivory moan my name. Along with the memory comes the anger.

Fuck her.

CHAPTER NINE

IVORY

Two months later...

"ARE YOU SURE YOU'RE OKAY?"

Megan holds my hair back as I vomit for the third time after stopping for a break. We have one more day of rafting before the trip is over. The rapids were extremely rough today due to the strong winds and the torrential downpour we had last night. Everyone is tired and sore from navigating the river.

"Yeah, I'm good." I straighten and wipe my mouth with the paper towel Megan hands me. "The current was stronger than I was expecting. All that bouncing around... I don't remember the last time it was that bad."

"It was a few years ago," Megan confirms. "I don't remember you getting sick, though."

I laugh. "No, last time I held *your* hair back."

Megan snaps her fingers. "That's right. I guess this is payback."

"I've been saving up."

"Obviously," she deadpans.

"At least it's not raining today."

"True," she says and points to the other rafters. "And you're not the only one who's turned a nasty shade of green."

I glance over to see several of our guests holding their stomachs. Kiera is dry-heaving next to another guy. I can't tell if it's because she was affected by the ride or if it's seeing other people getting sick. Either way, it's nice to know I'm not alone.

"Alright, everyone!" I holler. "Let's get our tents put up and a fire started so we can hunker down for the night. Then we can start dinner."

"Heifer, it's been over a week, and you still look like shit," Eric criticizes.

I narrow my brows. "Thanks for your opinion, Queenie."

Megan's head shoots up from her computer. "He's not wrong, Ivory. Maybe you caught a bug on the rapids trip. You haven't felt good for a while now. Go to the doctor."

"You know I hate doctors," I state firmly.

"What's wrong with doctors?" Eric asks, his lashes fluttering. "Some of them are yummy to look at while they lean in close to examine *every single inch* of you."

"Gross!" Megan complains. "Don't make me tell RaRa you're thinking about other men."

"Wench!" Eric screeches. "Believe me when I say that that man covers all my needs, but I'm not dead. I can enjoy a nice specimen if I see one. Looky, but no touchy."

I roll my eyes. "Doctors mean needles. Needles are the devil and a hard pass."

Eric gasps. "Girl, you put your life on the line daily for the thrill of the adrenaline rush, but needles still send you running for the hills?"

Megan laughs. "Yep! Last time she went to the doctor was because we needed a physical for life insurance policies. The lab tech came in to draw blood, and *Ms. Chase the High* over there, fainted."

"It was a big fucking needle!" I shout. I grab my purse out of my drawer and stand up. "Fine, I'll go to the doctor, but you two are dicks!"

Laughter follows me out of the office as I stomp through the lobby. Little do they know, I already have an appointment. Who knows what I could have picked up to make me feel so horrible? Parasites come to mind as I pull into my primary care's parking lot.

After getting checked in, the nurse escorts me to one of the bathrooms.

"Let's get a urine sample first," she says, handing me a plastic cup. "Then we'll see what Dr. Hardy says after her exam and any other tests she might want."

"Okay." I take the cup and do my business, placing it behind the metal door on the wall when I'm done. Once I step into the hallway, the nurse beckons me to follow her to the exam room.

A few minutes later, Dr. Hardy bursts in. "Ah, Ivory, my favorite patient. To what do I owe this pleasure?" Dr. Hardy winks. "Is it time for another physical?"

Dr. Hardy has been my doctor for years, and she knows I won't willingly come to see her unless my hand is forced.

I really hate fucking needles.

"Um... no... nothing like that."

Dr. Hardy looks down at my chart. "I'm teasing you, but just a heads up, we might have to draw blood today."

I blanch. "I have faith in your abilities, so we definitely won't need to do that."

Dr. Hardy smirks. "When did your symptoms start?"

I quickly explain how I got sick a week ago, on the yearly camping trip, and how bad the rapids were. I also tell her that I'm still nauseous, dizzy, and tired.

"Could I have a parasite?" I ask nervously.

Dr. Hardy narrows her gaze. "What have I told you about WebMD?"

"To stay away from it."

"Let's go ahead and get started." She pokes and prods around my mouth, nose, and ears before making me lie down on the crinkly paper-covered exam table. Dr. Hardy pushes around on my stomach. "Does this hurt?"

"No," I say, while silently thanking God it doesn't and for not hurling all over her shoes.

Dr. Hardy tugs my hand to help me sit back up. The room spins around me, and I close my eyes, breathe deeply through my nose, and exhale through my mouth.

"Dizzy?"

"I got up too fast, I think."

"Hmm."

Before I can ask what she's thinking, a knock on the door interrupts us.

The nurse rushes forward and gives Dr. Hardy a piece of paper. "Here're Ms. Whitman's urine results."

She studies it for a moment before a smile spreads across her face.

"I take it by that smile on your face, I passed, and it's good news," I say, relieved.

"Yes, I'd say it's good news, but also possibly bad news."

My heart hammers in my chest. "What's the bad news?"

"We're gonna have to draw some blood today."

"Fuck," I mutter. "If that's the bad news, what the hell could possibly be the good news?"

"I'd like to take some blood to be a hundred percent accurate, but judging on the levels of your HCG, you're pregnant. Congratulations!"

"No… no… no," I deny. "That can't be right. I'm on the shot."

Dr. Hardy's smile falls. "Ivory, you know that any type of birth control, other than abstinence, isn't fool-proof. Have you missed a shot?"

"I was a week late getting it a couple of months ago, but I didn't miss it."

"I take it this wasn't planned then?" she asks. I

shake my head vigorously. "Even missing a dosage for a couple of days in between your schedule can result in ovulation.

"I'm always careful."

"I'm not saying you aren't," she replies gently. "Before we go off the deep end, I'm gonna have Jill come in and draw some blood. I'll be back once I have the results.

Jill has me lie back down on the table due to my history of fainting while she preps to take blood. Numbness spreads through my body, and I'm so focused on Dr. Hardy's words, *'You're pregnant'*, that I don't even register the needle going into my arm.

"All done." Jill pats my arm. "Do you want me to help you sit up, or do you want to lay here for a while?"

"I'm fine here," I respond.

"Dr. Hardy will be back soon."

There's no way I'm pregnant. The urine test has to be wrong.

When Dr. Hardy comes back in about twenty minutes later, her expression shows no sign of what the tests are.

"Was the urine test wrong?" I ask pleadingly.

Dr. Hardy's eyes soften with remorse. "I'm sorry, Ivory. You're pregnant."

"I-I-I can't be," I stutter.

"The blood test confirms it," she explains, looking back down at her notes. "I can't guess how far along you are due to you being on the shot. Do you know when this could have happened?"

Only one night comes to mind because I haven't been with anyone since Purgatory. Before that, it'd been months since I broke up with Keith.

Spike.

It's a good thing I'm still lying on the exam table because my world suddenly tilts on its axis, and blackness engulfs me.

"Ivory, open your eyes," a voice commands. "Come on, you can do it."

I slowly peel open my eyelids, blinking the room into focus. "What happened? Where am I?"

"There she is," Dr. Hardy says as she looms over me, shining a light in my eyes.

I flinch away from the light as everything that's happened barrels forward in my mind.

Purgatory, a one-night stand with Spike, the camping trip, and Dr. Hardy telling me I'm pregnant. Please, please, please let this be a dream.

A single tear runs down the side of my face as it all hits me all over again.

Someone squeezes my hand, and I slowly turn my head to see Megan sitting next to me, her brows pinched with concern. I slowly sit up, hating that I look vulnerable.

"Easy, Ivory," Dr. Hardy warns. "Nice and slow."

"What are you doing here?" I ask Megan, but it's Dr. Hardy who answers.

"You fainted," Dr. Hardy explains. "We called your emergency contact."

"You're okay," Megan reassures me once she's sure I'm going to remain upright. "You should've told me you were coming to the doctor. We both know how you are when they break out the needles."

That's all it takes for the waterworks to start. Sobs wrack my body as Megan jumps up and pulls me closer to her.

"Ivory, what's wrong?"

"I'm going to leave you two alone now. Ivory, I don't want you driving the rest of the day. You need to rest," Dr. Hardy commands as she opens the door.

"Don't worry, Doc," Megan answers, rubbing my back. "I'll take care of her."

After the door closes, I pull away from Megan's embrace. "I'm pregnant," I blurt, knowing it's the last thing she's expecting me to say.

Megan steps back, shock registering in her eyes, and scans my face. "What did you say?"

"Please don't make me say it again," I beg. "Megan, what am I going to do?"

"Do you know who the father is?" she asks as I glare at her. "You know I didn't mean it like that. I know you were with Spike that one time, but I didn't know if you moved on and were seeing someone else."

"I fucking wish I could tell you that," I reply, chuckling bitterly. "Unfortunately, no, this is all Spike."

"You don't have to go through this alone if you decide to keep it," she says softly. "I'll be the greatest auntie in the world, and Eric is going to go nuts. But you don't have to decide now."

I grimace. "Spike's the father. He has a right to know before I make any decisions."

"Call him," she encourages.

"I can't. We didn't exactly exchange numbers."

Megan taps her chin in thought. "Wait a couple of days and go find him at Purgatory. At least you know the club owns it, and they're there all the time."

"No," I say firmly. "I need to do this today, or I'll lose my nerve."

"Alright," she hesitates. "I'll drive you."

"I have to do this myself."

"You heard the doctor," she argues. "You can't drive. In fact, you're supposed to rest." Megan holds up her hand to silence me when I open my mouth to protest. "I'll stay in the car, but I'll be damned if you do this alone."

"Fine, let's go," I concede.

Forty-five minutes later, we pull up outside of Purgatory. It's only five-thirty, and it doesn't appear too busy yet. I grip my purse and say a silent prayer as I reach for the door handle.

"I can go in with you," Megan offers again.

"I love you, but I have to handle this on my own." I slip one leg out of the car. "You got your phone?"

"Always," she promises.

"I'll text you if I need rescuing," I joke, trying to ease the tension.

"Good luck," she calls as I shut the door.

It takes a minute for my eyes to adjust once I'm inside. I scan the floor but only see a couple of members of Saint Purgatory, none of whom are Spike. I take a relieved breath.

I'm not as ready for this conversation as I thought.

"Ivory!" Skye hollers from the bar. I walk over and take a seat in front of her. "Haven't seen you in a while. Did we scare you and your friends off? RaRa won't quit gabbing about Eric," she gushes without taking a breath.

I giggle. "Eric won't shut up about him either."

"So, where's your posse?"

"I'm alone," I lie. "Is Spike here today?"

An unreadable look crosses her features, but before I can ask her what it's about, she responds. "No, he had some club business to take care of and probably won't be in."

My shoulders slump. "Do you have his number?"

Skye fidgets behind the counter, her face at war with itself. "I'm not supposed to give out the guys' numbers."

"Oh."

"It's not that I don't wa—"

"It's okay," I reassure her. "I understand. I'm basically a stranger, and you're looking out for them."

"You can give me your number, and I'll make sure he gets it."

"That'd be great, thank you."

Skye slides her phone across the bar. "Here, put it in my phone, if you're okay with that, so I don't lose it." I type my number into her phone, and she sends me a text after I hand it back. "Now you have my number, too. Can I get you anything to drink?"

"I better head back home, no DD tonight." I slide off the stool. "Thanks again for giving him my number."

Skye waves. "See ya soon?"

I shrug. "We'll see."

Before she can ask any more questions, I spin on my heel and head for the door.

Ball's in your court, Spike.

CHAPTER TEN

SPIKE

"C'MON, YOU CAN DO BETTER THAN THAT."

I bounce on the balls of my feet and watch Grim's hands carefully. Sparring with him is always fun because we don't use boxing gloves or anything so we can freely sign. Sure, his face typically gives away the important stuff, but I'm not taking any chances.

"Don't want to hurt you," I counter with a smirk.

His brows shoot up. "You really think you could hurt me? Bro, I'm like twice your size and twice as mean."

"They don't call you the Grim Reaper for nothing."

He throws a right hook, and I dodge it easily.

"C'mon, you can do better than that," I mock, shifting from side to side.

His cheeks redden with anger, but I'm fairly certain the emotion is directed at himself. It's not like him to miss.

"What're you so pissed off about, anyway?" he asks.

Oh, I don't know. How about the fact that I haven't been laid in over a month, and the one chick I want has ghosted me.

"I'm not pissed," I lie.

"You know we're gonna get that Carter guy, right?" he signs, referring to the child abuser who's still in a jail cell instead of six feet under.

"I know Carmella's doing everything she can," I reply. Abyss's old lady is an amazing attorney, but the justice system isn't always as *cooperative* as we need it to be. "But she's not God. She might not be able to work her legal magic."

Grim scowls before lunging at me. This time, he lands a punch, and I'm knocked to the floor. He stares at me for a moment, then thrusts his hand out to help me to my feet.

"We'll get him," he insists. "But I don't think it's Carter who's got you all in knots."

Damn him and his ability to read people.

"Don't know what you mean."

It's my turn to throw a punch, and even as strong as I am, the blow barely moves him. I growl with rage and start to deliver punch after punch to Grim's torso. And the fucking idiot simply stands there and takes it.

When I'm finished, and my breathing is erratic, he turns to walk to the bench and sit.

"Now that you got that outta the way," he signs. "What the fuck is really going on?"

I stare at him for a few minutes, trying to gather my thoughts. Rather than give him an explanation, I storm out of the gym. I make my way to the common room, but before I can reach the bar, Skye steps in front of me.

"Where ya goin'?" she asks, crossing her arms over her chest.

I'm tapped on the shoulder, so I glance back and see Grim glaring at me. "Did you really think that walking away from me would stop me from giving a damn?"

Throwing my hands up, I step to the side so I can face them both. "Grim, I don't want to fucking talk about it. Skye, I'm going to the bar."

Grim just shakes his head and stalks away toward the members' wing. Skye, on the other hand, continues to block my path.

"Ivory came looking for you tonight," she spits out.

My muscles tense to an almost painful degree. "Good for her," I snap.

I push past Skye, but her words stop me in my tracks. "Phew, thank fuck. I thought you were gonna be mad at me for not giving her your number."

Slowly turning back around, I narrow my eyes. "What?"

She shrugs. "She wanted your number, but I figured you wouldn't want me to give it to her."

"You saw her?" I ask, my voice betraying me and revealing my relief.

"Yeah." She smirks. "But you don't care about that."

"Skye," I growl. "What did she want?"

"I told you, your number."

"And you didn't give it to her?"

"I didn't." Her lips tilt into a grin. "But I got her's for you."

My shoulders slump. "Really?"

"Yes, really." Skye pulls her cell out of her back pocket and taps on the screen. "Just shared her contact info."

Turning on my heel, I break out into a run toward my room. Skye's laughter follows me all the way down the hall, but I don't give a damn. All I can focus on at the moment is getting a hold of Ivory and figuring out what the fuck I did to make her ghost me.

And all that's going to accomplish, idiot, is her thinking you're desperate.

When I reach my room and the door slides closed behind me, I take several deep breaths to calm myself. I grab my phone off my dresser and stare at the text from Skye before opening it and tapping on Ivory's number. Three rings seem more like a million.

"Hello."

Ivory's voice wraps around me like the steam from a sauna, easing all my aches and pains.

"You ran out on me," I blurt. Not exactly how I wanted to start this call, but here we are.

"Spike?"

I chuckle roughly and with zero humor. "So, you run out on so many guys that you can't keep them all straight."

"It's…" A rustling sound comes through the line. "Dammit, it's almost three in the morning."

"Your point?"

"It's late, Spike," she says with a sigh. "Did you need something?"

"You're the one who came looking for me."

"Right. But maybe you could call back at a decent hour."

I could, but I'm not caving that easily. Besides, she answered. If she didn't want to talk, she should've ignored the call.

"I'm good now."

"Okay, fine. I wanted to talk to you beca—"

"Why'd you take off that morning?" I demand. "You ashamed to have fucked a biker?"

"What? No!"

"Coulda fooled me," I gripe. "Ya know, I knew I was only a dare to you, but I wasn't expecting you to be an uptight bitch."

Without warning, the call is disconnected.

Yeah. I went too far.

CHAPTER ELEVEN
IVORY

"Asshole!"

I grip my phone tight, ready to throw it across the room.

How fucking dare he! We agreed no strings attached, no commitment. Just two adults throwing caution to the wind and indulging in a good time with a complete stranger.

I storm out of my bedroom to pace around the living room, huffing and puffing. There's only one person I can turn to at this hour. I hit the number one contact in my cell and wait for her to answer.

"Hey, babe, ho—"

"Megan," I choke out.

"Ivory, what's wrong?" she demands, the sleep instantly vanishing from her voice. "What happened?"

"Spike happened."

"Oookay," she draws out. "I'm gonna need specifics. I take it he got your message and called."

"Yep." I laugh sardonically. "All he cared about was why I ran out on him. And he called me an uptight bitch."

"Did he really call you an uptight bitch?" Megan asks quietly, her tone deadly.

That's one of the things I love about her. She's protective to a fault and extremely loyal to those she loves.

"Sure did," I confirm. "I don't need or want anything from that dickface. I never want to see him again."

"That might be kinda tough… You're pregnant with his kid."

"So? There are single parents everywhere, and if they can make it work, so can I."

"Hard to do if he pursues visitation rights," she counters. "He might want to be a part of his kid's life."

"We never discussed me being pregnant," I admit.

"You didn't tell him?" Megan is silent for a beat. "Ivory, maybe this is all just a big misunderst—"

"I told you what he said to me!"

"Hun, I'm on your side," she says gently. "You've had a shock today. Maybe if you sleep on it, you'll fe—"

"No," I say stubbornly. "He proved to me during our phone call the kind of man he is. The baby and I don't need him in our lives. We'll have you and Eric. You're more than enough."

"If that's really how you feel, you know we'll support you a hundred percent."

"It is," I confirm. "I've gotta go. I'm getting a headache."

The weight of the world crashes on my shoulders as I bite my lip to keep from crying. I can't afford to fall apart until I hang up. Megan will get in her car and force her way in to take care of me, and right now, I want to be alone. I don't want to see the judgment in her eyes. It's bad enough I can hear it in her voice. I know deep down she'll follow my lead, but for now, I need space to think.

"Alright," Megan agrees. "I *am* here for you. I support whatever you want. Get some rest, and I'll check on you tomorrow. Love you."

"Love you."

I disconnect the call and fall onto the couch in a heap, finally allowing the sobs to wrack my body. I tuck my knees into my chest and reach for a pillow as I wrap myself tight in a throw blanket.

Bang. Bang. Bang.

I roll over, reaching for the remote to turn the television off. How did I fall asleep with the volume up that loud? My body hits the floor with a thud before I realize that I'm not in my bed. I groan as I scramble to untangle myself and stand on shaky legs. The banging continues, and it hits me that it's coming from the front door. My head snaps towards the unwelcome intrusion.

I stomp toward the sounds, unlock the door, and throw it open. "Megan, I to—"

Spike has his fist raised ready to pound on my door again. "Not Megan," he says gruffly.

"Obviously," I snap. "What do you want, Spike? And how the fuck did you know where I live?"

"I wanna talk, and to answer your second question, not a lot of Ivorys around these parts."

"I tried to talk to you before you barked at me earlier, or did you already forget calling me an uptight bitch?" I hiss. "You need to go. We have nothing else to say to each other."

I attempt to slam the door in his face, but Spike's hand shoots out and stops it.

"Ivory, please," he pleads. "I know I was a dick to you earlier, and you have no reason to let me in, but hear me out."

I take a deep breath, fully intending to deny his request. But then I remember the baby I'm carrying and sigh.

"Fine." I step back and gesture for him to enter. "You have five minutes."

CHAPTER TWELVE

SPIKE

You have five minutes.

I'm not entirely sure I can say what's on my mind in that amount of time, but I'm inside, and that's a giant step in the right direction.

"Time's ticking," she snipes as she paces the length of her living room.

I watch her every move, and my eyes are drawn to her face. Her eyes are puffy, and she looks exhausted.

"Are you okay?" I ask.

She stops in her tracks and spins to glare at me. "Like you give a damn."

"I know you won't believe me, but I *do* care. I'm not a monster."

"Coulda fooled me."

Thrusting my fingers through my hair, I close the distance between us and grab her arm with my free hand. "C'mon. Sit down," I urge.

Surprisingly, she doesn't resist, but she does sit as far away from me as her couch will allow. I take in the pillow and rumpled blanket, and guilt surges through me.

"Why'd you sleep on the couch?" I ask.

"What makes you think I did?"

I tilt my head. "Ivory, I'm not stupid."

She huffs out a breath. "Fine. I was pissed after you called me an uptight bitch, so I decided to watch true crime documentaries to help me plot your murder."

I chuckle, and for the first time since arriving, I feel a little lighter. "Learn anything good?"

A ghost of a smile graces her lips. "Yep. You should be careful because you might not make it outta here alive."

"I'll keep that in mind."

Ivory relaxes slightly and curls her legs under her. "Why are you here, Spike?"

"Because I wanted to talk to you."

"You made it pretty clear how you feel about me on the phone," she snaps. "What more is there to say?"

"I'm sorry about that."

"Okay, fine. Apology accepted." She glances toward the door. "You can leave now."

"Why'd you come looking for me at Purgatory?" I

ask, ignoring her obvious desire for me to leave her alone. Her only response is to shrug. "C'mon, Ivory. You must've had a reason."

"I don't remember."

"Damn, you're stubborn." I grin. "That's kinda hot."

Without warning, she grabs a pillow and launches it at my head. I swat it before it hits me.

"Spike, I'm really tired," she says with a sigh. "Can you just get to your point? Please?"

"Fine. I wanted to apologize for calling you an uptight bitch, which I've already done." I scoot closer to her and brush a blonde strand of hair out of her face. "And I just wanted to see you again."

Her eyes snap to mine. "You did?"

"Yeah. I mean, I enjoyed our night together. But then you left, and I thought…" I shake my head. "Well, it doesn't matter what I thought. We clearly weren't on the same page."

Ivory stares at me, her chocolate eyes swimming with some unidentifiable emotion. "I don't do one-night stands, Spike. That night with you… It was way out of character for me."

"Was it? Because I remember a girl who made it clear she doesn't back down from a dare. And I also remember that you had zero complaints while we were at that motel."

"Okay, so I don't back down from a dare," she concedes. "Problem is, my heart and soul do. I'm not looking for a relationship, certainly not from a—"

"Biker," I snap bitterly. "Yeah, you've made that clear." I stare at her imploringly. "Then why'd you come looking for me?"

"Because…" Ivory shrugs. "I don't know. I had fun with you, that's all."

"And what? You were hoping for a repeat performance?"

Please say yes.

"Yes. No." She sighs. "I don't know."

"Well, which is it?"

"Look, just forget you ever met me, okay?"

"Not likely."

Ivory shifts to sit on the edge of the cushion and picks her cell up off the coffee table. "Dammit. I, uh, gotta get ready for work."

I see right through her attempt to politely dismiss me and decide to give in… for now. "Okay."

She stands and walks to the door. "Um… give me a call later, and we can talk some more."

"You won't hang up on me this time?"

"Depends." She opens the front door. "Now, I really do need you to go. I've gotta get movin'."

Rising to my feet, I nod and stride to the door. "I'll call you later."

"Right. Goodbye, Spike."

She shuts the door as soon as I'm over the threshold, and at this moment, I know she won't answer my call.

Doesn't mean I won't try.

CHAPTER THIRTEEN

IVORY

Two weeks later...

"Next!"

I swallow the lump in my throat and step toward the receptionist, wishing I would've let Megan come with me.

Woulda, coulda, shoulda. Stupid, stubborn ass pride.

"I-I-Ivory Whitman." I clear my throat and steady my nerves. "I have an appointment with Dr. Wilde."

The woman types feverishly on the computer before asking for my insurance card which I promptly hand over.

She grins at me as she takes it. "I see you're here for your first OB appointment. You look nervous."

"That obvious, huh?" I joke. The nametag on her scrubs says *Aubrey*. "You have a beautiful name."

Aubrey blushes. "Thank you." She hands back

my insurance information. "I take it this is your first baby."

"Yeah."

"Don't worry," she reassures. "This is a great office, and Dr. Wilde is one of the best."

"Thanks, I needed to hear that."

She hands me a stack of papers attached to a clipboard. "Fill these out and give them to your nurse when you're done. You'll be fine, you'll see."

I nod and take the paperwork. I find an empty seat and start filling out the forms. After fifteen minutes, I have to stop and shake the cramps from my fingers.

This could seriously be a new torture method. Who the hell needs all this information?

My breath catches when I reach *Name of Father* on the information sheet. The blank line mocks me, daring me to lie. With a shaky hand, I scribble *Hunter Long*. I don't have his address, and I'm not about to give anyone his number so I leave the rest of his information blank.

"Ivory Whitman," a nurse calls. I grab my things and hurry to follow her. "My name's Paula. How are you today?"

Paula has a calming presence about her that automatically puts me at ease. "Good. Nervous, I guess."

"That's normal, but don't worry. We'll explain

everything to you, and feel free to ask as many questions as you need to."

"Okay."

Paula stops in front of a scale. "We need to get a starting weight so we can monitor your progress through the pregnancy, and then we'll get a urine sample."

I slip off my shoes before stepping onto the scale. "Another urine sample?" I ask. "Didn't Dr. Hardy forward my test results?"

"She did," Paula confirms as she writes. "However, you're pregnant, and unfortunately, you'll be peeing a lot. We just need to make sure it's from the pregnancy and not from a UTI. You'll be asked to give a sample each time you come in to be sure."

"Okay." I slide my shoes back on. "As long as they're no needles."

"Oh, we'll be getting some blood today before you leave."

I stumble as soon as the word blood leaves her mouth.

Definitely should've let Megan come with me.

Paula's hand shoots out to steady me before I faceplant. "Did you say blood?"

Paula smiles. "I take it you're not a fan of blood."

"Blood doesn't bother me. Needles bother me."

She pats my arm and leads me to an open room.

"I promise our lab tech is very gentle. Is Dad out in the waiting room? We can bring him back."

I shake my head. "My best friend was going to come, but something came up at work," I lie.

"Tell you what, I'll have them tell me when it's time, and I'll come back in and hold your hand."

"You don't have to." I blow out a frustrated breath. "I'm gonna be a mom. Time to put on my big girl panties and get over the fear."

"It's not a problem." She slips the blood pressure cuff on my arm. "To tell you the truth, most women who come in here hate needles."

"Really?"

"Yep. In fact, you're not my first one today."

I giggle. "That makes me feel better."

"Your blood pressure is a little elevated. Do you normally run high?"

"Nope, that's your fault," I accuse, and her eyes widen in surprise. "You said the word needle."

Paula laughs. "Well, if that's all it takes, we'll come up with a code word."

"Perfect."

"Dr. Wilde will be right in."

"Thank you."

"I'll be back when the tech comes in," she says as she opens the door.

Seconds later, Dr. Wilde appears.

"Hello, I'm Dr. Wilde." She holds her hand out for me to shake.

"Ivory," I respond.

"Let's get to it, shall we?" she says before opening her laptop. "Is this your first pregnancy?"

"Yes."

"Congratulations!"

"Thank you."

I've come to terms with being pregnant, but fear still swirls in my gut. Will I be a good mom? Can I do this on my own? I know I have Eric and Megan in my corner, but it's not the same as the baby having its father in its life.

Dr. Wilde studies me. "Judging by the look on your face, I'd say this was a shock."

"You could say that," I mumble.

She squeezes my hand. "We'll get you through it. I'm sure Paula told you that we will explain everything that is happening as it comes up?"

"She did. She's great."

"I'd be lost without her," she says fondly. "Ask as many questions as you need to. If you can't think of any now, you can always call, and we *will* call you back."

"That's good to know because my mind is a jumbled mess right now."

She winks. "We get that a lot here. Today, all

we're going to do is an ultrasound and some other tests, along with your medical history."

"Isn't it too early for an ultrasound?"

"It is for an external one, but we're going to do an internal one."

"Internal?"

"I'll insert a wand into your vagina and take some pictures."

"Does it hurt?" I ask.

"Not at all. You might feel some pressure, though," she explains. "When we're done, you'll have pictures of your little bundle to take home."

For the first time, excitement builds. "Okay, I'm ready."

Dr. Wilde completes my history and has Paula come back in when she performs the physical portion of the exam. The ultrasound doesn't hurt, but it is uncomfortable having another person jam a probe up my hoo-ha and wiggle it around.

Tears prick my eyes when Dr. Wilde turns the screen toward me. "There he or she is." She points to a blip on the screen. "See that fluttering?"

I nod because words are caught in my throat.

"That's the heartbeat."

"The heartbeat?" I whisper.

"Yes," Dr. Wilde confirms as she pulls the wand out. "You're right on track, and everything looks perfect. I'll print the pictures for you while you get yo—" Paula shakes her head, interrupting her. "Ah, I see. Okay, I'll leave the pictures up front for you to grab when you check out. And we'll see you in six weeks, but call if you need anything."

"Thank you, Dr. Wilde."

True to her word, Paula stands by my side, gripping my hand in hers, as the phlebotomist gets to work. My mind wanders back to the beautiful scene on the monitor, and I don't even feel the needle.

"All done!" Paula announces as she helps me up slowly, so I don't get dizzy when I stand. "I'll walk you out."

I follow her out, and she informs a different receptionist that I need an appointment for six weeks out and hands me the first pictures I'll ever have of my baby.

My baby. I'm having a baby.

After making the appointment, I walk out of the office and am oblivious to the world around me as I make my way to my car.

"What the fuck do you think you're playing at?" a shrill voice says from behind me.

I spin around, clutching my heart and almost dropping my precious photos in the process.

"Aubrey?" It takes a minute for my brain to catch up with who spoke. "Did I forget something?"

"You have some gall putting Hunter Long down as the father of your bastard baby."

"W-w-what are you talking about?" I stammer.

There's no way she knows who Spike is. This is just a coincidence, right? Plenty of people have the name Hunter Long.

"Hunter Long… Spike," she confirms. The blood in my veins runs cold. "*My* fucking man."

"You're what?"

"My man!"

"This has to be a mistake."

"You listed Spike as the father, so either you're lying, or you fucked my old man."

"I-I-I didn't know. I promise." I hold up my hands in surrender. "He never said he was taken. I never wou—"

"Honey," she says condescendingly. "Spike's a biker. What did you expect? You were just another wet hole for him. You weren't his first and won't be his last."

"And you're okay with that?" My voice wobbles, but I stand firm.

Aubrey smirks. "I know the score. Bikers aren't known for being monogamous." She narrows her eyes. "What I want to know is what you want from him."

"Nothing, absolutely nothing." I hold her gaze so she can see the truth in my eyes.

She snorts. "I find that hard to believe."

"It's true," I affirm. "I haven't even told him I'm pregnant."

Her face flashes with a look I can't decipher before she puts her mask back in place. "That's probably a good idea… for your sake."

"Why?" I'm genuinely curious as to what she's going to say.

"Seeing how he's *mine*, I fuck him every night," she explains. "In fact…" Aubrey places her hands on her stomach, and my heart drops. It makes sense, though. If she's his old lady, of course, they're having sex.

Aubrey is having his baby, too. My child will have a brother or sister out there they'll never know about.

My mind swirls with the information Aubrey hurled at me as saliva pools in my mouth, and my stomach somersaults. I bend over, hands on my knees, as I lose my lunch.

"Gross," Aubrey says as she steps back. "Spike's not gonna want to raise your bastard when he has *our* baby to take care of." She eyes my stomach. "I'd keep *that* little secret to yourself, Ivory. You don't have the backbone for the biker lifestyle."

I wipe my mouth off. "I have no intention of

telling Spike about this baby," I vow. "I don't want anything else to do with him, I promise."

She spins on her heel, leaving without another word.

I knew he was a no-good lying piece of shit. That mother fucker better hope I never see him again, or I'll rip his dick off myself.

CHAPTER FOURTEEN

SPIKE

"THERE YOU ARE."

I kick my leg over the seat of my Harley and turn to face Glitter. Stifling my groan, I start toward the elevator.

"Here I am."

"We need to talk, Spike," she blurts, trying to keep up with me.

"'Bout what?"

She hesitates and wrings her hands while we wait for the elevator to arrive at the above-ground clubhouse garage. "Um… maybe we can talk in private?"

I glance around the large space. "We're alone, Glitter. Doesn't get much more private than that."

"Call me Aubrey."

Immediately, the hairs on the back of my neck stand on end. No way a bunny wants to be called by their real name unless they want something they know a biker isn't willing to give easily.

"Why would I do that?"

The elevator door slides open, and we both step inside. Neither of us talk as we descend to the common room, and it's her who finally breaks the silence.

"Please, Spike," she pleads. "I need to talk to you."

I take a deep breath. "Fine," I say, making my way to one of the tables in the corner and knowing she'll follow. "What is it?" I ask when we're both seated.

"I'm…" More hand wringing. "I'm pregnant."

Not what I was expecting.

"And you're telling me beca—"

"You're the father," she blurts.

"Bullshit," I bark. "You're a fucking club bunny, Glitter. Mine is hardly the only cock you've ridden."

She frantically shakes her head as she reaches into her purse and pulls out what appear to be several pictures. Glitter thrusts them at me. "See," she says, pointing to the first picture. "There's a picture of the sonogram. It's your baby, Spike."

No, no, no!

I glare at the image, silently willing it to burst into flames. "Doesn't prove it's mine."

"I haven't slept with anyone since you," she insists.

Thinking back over the last several weeks, I try to conjure up a memory of her slinking off with one of my brothers, but I come up empty.

Fuck.

"How far along are you?" I ask, hoping there's still a way outta this.

"Almost eight weeks."

Doing the math, I realize that she's right. It's likely my kid.

Double fuck.

"Anyway, I wanted you to know," she says, interrupting my thoughts. "And I thought… Well…"

"You thought what?"

"Since I'm having your baby, I thought you'd want to… I don't know… get hitched or something."

I laugh bitterly. "Get hitched?" I repeat. "That's not how this is gonna work."

"Then how will it work?" she demands, jumping to her feet. "I'm not having an abortion."

I rear back at her words. "And I didn't say anything about that. You're gonna do what you're gonna do. If you have it, I'll support it."

"It's a person, not a thing."

"You know what I mean." I heave a sigh. "Glitter, you and me… We're not a thing. But I won't be an absent dad. You have my word on that."

Triple fuck. I'm tied to her forever now.

"We'd be good together, Spike. Real good."

"Never gonna happen."

"Never say never," she quips, an odd grin curving her lips.

"Never," I reiterate, my tone lethal.

Glitter turns to walk away. "We'll see," she says over her shoulder.

Lifting the sonogram pictures and staring at them, my mind races. Of course, this is my luck. Just when I felt like I might have a chance with Ivory, Glitter fucks it up.

Okay, fine. Maybe I don't stand a chance in hell with Ivory, but a man can dream, right?

Fuck, fuck, fuckity fuck.

CHAPTER FIFTEEN

IVORY

"Alright, we've got a lot to discuss today."

Megan stands at the head of the conference room table, waiting for the side conversations to die down. We have three part-time employees: Jackie, Dale, and Stacy. Milton and Jeremy are full-time, along with Megan and me. We called everyone in today for an impromptu round table discussion, so this should be an interesting staff meeting.

There'll be so many questions I'm not ready to answer.

I stand and clear my throat. "Thank you all for coming in today, even though most of you had the day off."

"Everything okay, boss?" Milton asks.

Stacy shifts in her chair. "Yeah, we're not all getting fired, are we?"

Megan shakes her head. "No, and we didn't mean to frighten anyone by calling you in today."

"I'm pregnant," I blurt.

All eyes focus on me. It's deathly quiet for what seems like an eternity before everyone starts cheering and rushing out of their chairs to embrace me and offer their congratulations.

Megan smiles warmly. "Okay, okay… Give Ivory some room to breathe. We still need to talk about the changes coming your way."

That silences the room, and everyone takes their seat again.

"Don't worry," I reassure. "Basically, what this means going forward is that I'll be taking a more administrative role in the office. I'll still do activities, but it'll be the less strenuous ones. Also, I'll chip in with pickups and dropoffs, as well as setting up campsites and whatever else I'm able to do.

"That being said," Megan picks up. "We'll need one or two of you to pick up extra hours if possible. We're in our busy season, and we'd rather give you all first pick to work more than hire new staff."

"We're family at *Chase the High*," I state. "This place runs like a well-oiled machine, and it'll be hard bringing in new blood and training them. However, if no one can take more hours, we understand. There will be no fallout if you can't."

Dale raises his hand. "Can we all get more hours added? Spread the love between all of us?"

"Yeah," Jackie agrees. "I could do some extra hours on weekends and after my classes are over."

"Me, too," Stacy says.

Milton waves his hand between him and Jeremy. "We can do overtime if you need us to."

Jeremy lifts his chin in solidarity.

Tears well in my eyes. These people are too good to be true. I don't know why I was so worried. They've all stepped up whenever we asked for extra help, but this is different. This isn't just for an excursion or two, this is for months.

"You guys do realize that this isn't just for a week or two?" I ask, giving voice to my thoughts. "We'll need the help from now until I give birth. Megan will need all hands on deck when I'm on maternity leave, as well."

"Yes," they all respond in unison.

"Do you know what you're having?" Jackie asks.

"Not yet." I grin. "Too early to tell. Besides, I don't know if I want to know or not."

"What does Daddy think about that?" Dale teases.

My body goes rigid. I blink rapidly, too afraid to tell them the truth about their boss having a one-night stand with a man who's in a committed relationship.

They'll never look at me the same. I'll be a slut in their eyes.

"Ivory will bring the baby in to visit after he or she is born," Megan says, changing the line of conversation and allowing me to avoid Dale's question.

Everyone must sense the tension because the subject of the baby's parentage isn't mentioned again. We finish outlining what new schedules will look like and various duties that will be assigned depending on the availability of those who have experience in the activities we offer. Some customers will be rescheduled to different days to accommodate, but we won't have to cancel anything for the foreseeable future at least.

A couple of hours later, I'm dead on my feet. The baby is an energy sucker, for sure.

Megan links her arm with mine as we make our way back to our office. "Want me to pick up some Chinese and meet you at your house?"

"Can we get dumplings, crab rangoon, spring rolls, sweet and sour chicken, and Mu Shu Pork?" I ask hopefully, suddenly ravenous.

"Damn, someone is hungry."

I nudge her in the ribs. "Hey, I'm eating for two."

Megan laughs. "Don't worry, that's my niece or nephew in there. I'll make sure you get your fix."

My stomach rumbles. "On second thought, you might want to double that order."

CHAPTER SIXTEEN

SPIKE

"SHE GOT IT DONE."

Cheers erupt around the table. We've been in church for only a few minutes, but Soul's news quickly changes the entire mood in the room.

"Seriously?" Abyss says. "You doubted my woman?"

"Chill the fuck out, man," Soul says with a laugh. "No one doubted Carmella. We knew she'd come through, but even you gotta admit, it took longer than we expected."

"And Carter Maxwell will be in our clutches within the week," Abyss snaps. "Not only did she get him within our reach, she got the charges thrown out on a technicality so we don't have to contend with cops at all."

"Yeah, yeah," I comment. "Mel's incredible. No one said she isn't."

"Moving on," Malice says. "We need to plan how we're gonna actually get the guy."

For the next hour, we toss around idea after idea until a solid plan of action is in place. Soul rises from his chair, and I know he's about to dismiss church, but I can't let that happen. Not yet.

"I've got one more thing," I say, standing, and Soul shifts his gaze to me. "If that's okay with you, Prez?"

He sweeps his hand. "The floor is yours."

I move to stand behind my chair and grip the back of it until my knuckles are white. "I, um, have some news."

"You're not dying, are you?" Grim signs, his movements agitated.

"What? No."

"Fifty bucks," he counters.

Groaning, I lift my hands, so I don't get another fine. "I'm not dying. Although, that might be preferable."

"Spit it out, already," Rogue demands. "Some of us have old lady's waiting on us to finish up here."

"Glitter's pregnant."

My eyes dart from one brother to the next until I've seen the shock in all of their expressions.

"Who's the father?" Possum asks.

"Dumb ass, he is," Thorn snaps before leveling his gaze on me. "Right?"

"Do you really think I'd be telling you this if I weren't?"

"Right. So…"

"I take it you're not happy about this," Soul says.

"Not at all."

"Didn't you use a rubber?" Abyss asks.

"Bro, the bunnies are supposed to be on the pill," I remind him, not that I should have to because he's the doctor who prescribes them all birth control. "Besides, I was wasted that night. She caught me in a weak moment."

"Listen, it doesn't matter how it happened," Malice adds and glances at me. "Making her your old lady isn't in the cards, is it?"

"Fuck no!"

"You won't abandon this child," Soul says with finality.

"Of course, I won't," I confirm hotly. "You know me better than that."

"You're right," Soul says. "What're ya gonna do?"

I thrust a hand through my hair. "I don't know. I mean, I'll step up, obviously. But I am not thrilled about the idea of being tied to Glitter for the rest of my life."

"Another fifty bucks," Grim signs.

"Fuck you," I grumble, and he only grins. "Maybe I could pay her off. She gives me the baby and goes her own way."

"A child needs a mother," Frenzy says from the other end of the table.

"And I've got all of you and plenty of women here to step in and help."

"Yes, you do," Soul confirms. "But maybe you should give this some more thought before doing anything you'll regret."

"Yeah. Yeah, okay."

I sit and tip my head back. I'll give it more thought alright. But there is no amount of pondering that's going to make me okay with this.

I'm not ready. And I fucking hate *Glitter.*

CHAPTER SEVENTEEN

IVORY

"Back again?"

Aubrey glares at me from behind her computer.

"Yes," I reply, my tone clipped.

Dr. Wilde is one of the best obstetricians in the area. Yes, I messed up by screwing Spike, but it takes two to tango. He shouldn't have stepped out on his old lady. I'm not going to quit getting the best care over a man. Aubrey and I only have to see each other here, so she's just gonna have to learn to deal with it.

"Have a seat," she says dismissively.

Paula calls me back fifteen minutes later. First stop, the dreaded scale. I step onto it and glare at the numbers as they go up.

Paula giggles when she notices my face. "Don't worry, this is a perfectly healthy weight gain for someone who's five months along."

"You're not the one who feels like they swallowed a basketball," I mumble.

For the past few months, no one would've known I was pregnant. I wasn't showing at all. It was great. But it didn't last. A couple of weeks ago, Peanut decided to make their existence known, and my stomach shot out like a beach ball.

"You know the drill." Paula hands me a plastic cup.

I do my business and meet her back in the hallway, where she leads me to the ultrasound tech. I decided I wanted to know the sex of the baby so I could prepare the nursery. Today, as long as Peanut cooperates, I'll know if I'm having a little prince or princess.

The tech greets me with a smile. "Hi, Ivory. My name's Gina. I'll be doing your ultrasound today."

"Hi," I reply.

She pats the exam table. "Hop up and tuck your shirt under your bra."

Luckily, the table isn't too high off the ground because there will definitely not be any hopping. I pull my shirt under my bra and wait for Gina to get situated.

"The gel has been in the warmer," she explains as she squirts it onto my protruding stomach. "Now, let's see this baby."

Gina moves the wand around, taking several different shots from different angles.

"Can you tell the sex?"

"If the baby cooperates, I can," she replies. "Do you want to know now, or do I need to write it down and put it in an envelope for later?"

"Now, please."

"Okay, let's see if the baby is willing to flash us."

I laugh as she fiddles around. My eyes seek out the screen. The baby's heart flutters, and one of the arms moves. I glance at the tech to ask her if she can see the gender yet. Her smile is replaced with a frown, and her eyebrows furrow in concentration.

"Is everything okay?"

Her smile slips back into place, but it doesn't reach her eyes. "I'll let Dr. Wilde tell you what the sex is."

"Okay." I sit up slowly and take notice that she never answered my question.

Gina leads me to one of the open exam rooms. "Dr. Wilde will be right with you."

She's gone before I can respond.

That was weird. She'd tell me if I was having twins, right?

No, not possible. I only saw one.

Yeah, like you're an expert.

I pace around the room while I wait for Dr. Wilde. It's another twenty minutes when a soft knock startles me.

"Hi, Ivory," Dr. Wilde greets and points to the chair next to the counter. "Have a seat. Sorry to keep you waiting."

Dr. Wilde's facial expression is the same as Gina's. Her smile's brittle, and her tone is too soft. It's almost as if she's approaching a wounded animal. Suddenly, I'm on edge. Anxiety creeps up my spine, goosebumps break out all over my arms, and I break out in a cold sweat.

"What's going on?" I demand.

Dr. Wilde's eyes soften as she sits next to me on her stool. "We found an abnormality during your ultrasound."

"Meaning?" My voice is barely above a whisper.

"The baby has a diaphragmatic hernia."

I grip the arms of the chair. "Omigod."

I have no idea what that means, but it sounds bad. My breathing becomes shallow, and it's almost impossible to suck air into my lungs.

"Ivory, I need you to calm down," Dr. Wilde coaxes. "Deep breaths... in through your nose, out through your mouth."

I follow her instructions until I can breathe normally again. Well, as normally as someone can when they're told something is wrong with their baby.

"What does that mean?" I ask as soon as I can form words again. "Diaphra... whatever you said."

"I won't sugarcoat it for you." Dr. Wilde spins the computer around and points to the ultrasounds. "Do you see that dark spot there?" I nod. "That's the hernia. Now, it can be life-threatening, but we caught it. Now we know what we'll face once the baby is born."

"It's treatable?"

"Yes. After he's born, we'll place an NG tube to feed him because he won't be able to eat on his own, and we'll also give him IV fluids. When he's a few days old, we will operate to repair the hernia," she explains. "He may need to be on a ventilator for a couple days after surgery, but we'll wean him off of it and slowly introduce bottle feeding. Once we know he's tolerating feeding and not having any issues going to the bathroom, he can be released. It'll probably be at least a week in the NICU."

"You're sure he needs surgery?" My lip quivers. "Isn't that dangerous?"

Dr. Wilde takes my hand. "With any surgery, there are dangers, but this is his best chance. This is treatable."

I can't freak out. I need to be strong for him.

Wait... what?

"I'm having a boy?"

Dr. Wilde grins for the first time since she entered the room. "Yes, you are. Congratulations!"

I rub my stomach as tears slip down my cheeks. "A little boy."

"A little boy," she confirms. "Everything else looks great. Next time you come in, we'll test you for gestational diabetes."

I stand and shake her hand. "You're sure he'll be okay?" I ask one last time.

"I promise we will take good care of both of you," Dr. Wilde responds. "There's no reason I can see that this won't be a normal pregnancy."

She never promised Peanut would be okay, only that she'd take care of both of us. I shudder at the thought of something possibly going wrong with the surgery and Spike never knowing he has a son.

Spike has a right to know he has a son and needs a life-saving operation when he's born. I can't be selfish anymore.

Mind made up, I check out and move to stand in front of Aubrey's computer. "Can you take a quick break? I need to talk to you."

She startles at my request but agrees to meet me outside.

"What do you want?" Aubrey huffs when she joins me in the parking lot.

I tell her everything that Dr. Wilde told me. "I

don't want to come between you and Spike," I tack on. "But he has a right to know that he's going to have a son who will need a major operation when he's born and how serious the situation is."

"You fucking liar," Aubrey sneers. "This is a ploy to get my man."

"I swear," I plead, holding up my hands. "I *do not* want Spike. I just feel he deserves to know."

"Let me explain something to you, homewrecker." Aubrey steps toward me, causing me to shuffle back. "Our men don't fuck around when it comes to their *real* family. They'll kill you before they let you ruin Spike's reputation with your lies."

"I'm not lying," I cry. "Dr. Wilde can confirm everything I said."

"Maybe, maybe not." Her eyes drop to my stomach. "Right now, though, there's no proof that that baby's even Spike's."

I rear back as if I've been slapped. "Spike's the only man I've been with in almost a year."

"The club will never believe that," she taunts. "It'll be your word against an old lady. Who do ya think they'll believe… a stupid little slut who had a one-night stand or me?" My shoulders slump in defeat. "If you don't want to end up dead before you give birth, I suggest you keep your fucking mouth shut. The next time you even think about talking to

Spike, remember this. I have pull with the club, you don't. One of us will be on the losing end of a bullet, and honey, it sure as hell won't be me."

I use my purse to shield my stomach. "Sorry, forget I said anything."

"We'll pretend this conversation never happened." She smirks. "I don't know you, and you sure as fuck don't know Spike."

"Right." I spin on my heel and run toward my car as her laughter follows me.

I was right, Saints Purgatory is bad news. Very bad news if they're willing to kill a pregnant woman carrying a member's baby.

Once I'm behind the wheel, I let the tears flow. I sit for a while before I start the engine.

At least I have Megan and Eric. They're all we need.

CHAPTER EIGHTEEN
SPIKE

"You don't find it suspicious at all?"

I down the rest of my beer before glancing at Possum. He's been yapping my ear off for the last hour about tattoos, so I've been tuning him out.

"What's suspicious?"

"Dude, look," he demands, and my eyes follow the trajectory of his arm to where he's pointing. "She's not even showing."

I stare at Glitter, who's walking across the room. I'd been so engrossed in ignoring Possum that I didn't even realize she'd gotten home from work.

Returning my attention to Possum, I shrug. "Not all women show much."

"True," he says. "But c'mon, brother. You've gotta admit that you've got concerns about her."

"Of course, I do," I snap, slamming my empty bottle onto the bar. "But it doesn't matter."

"Spike, listen to me," he orders. "I've been where

139

you're at. And trust me when I say, you want to get confirmation."

Slowly, I turn on my stool. "What do you mean, you've been where I'm at?"

He glances around the room as if determining whether he'll be overheard, and then he leans in close. "I'll deny this until the day I die, but a few years back, Candy thought she was pregnant. Told me it was mine."

I straighten. "Candy? Seriously?"

"Yep. Freaked right the fuck out," he admits. "Fortunately, Candy isn't psycho, and I went with her to the doctor to find out for sure. We could've had Abyss do the blood test, but we didn't want anyone to know. Anyway, she wasn't pregnant."

"How is that the same position as me?" I narrow my eyes. "And on what planet is she not psycho? We kicked her out because she's exactly that," I remind him.

"That's not the point."

"Then what is the point?"

"The point is this," he begins dramatically. "You have nothing proving that Glitter's baby is yours. Don't you think you should figure that out?"

"She said she didn't sleep with anyone after me."

"And you believe her?"

"Yeah, I guess."

"Do you really want to hang your entire future on 'I guess'?"

Possum's words play on repeat in my brain until my ire is all the way fucking up. I shoot to my feet and stomp across the common room toward the wing Glitter stays in. When I reach her door, I don't bother knocking. Rather, I use my palm print to open it, knowing that Jez and Fort set it up so all club officers can access every room in this wing. Our hands are a master key of sorts.

Glitter whirls around and glares at me. "What are you doing, Spike?"

"We need to talk."

She spreads her palm over her still flat stomach and smiles. "I like the sound of that."

"Sit down," I command. When she starts toward me, I hold up my hand. "Sit the hell down, Glitter."

Her smile falters as she slinks backward and sits on the edge of her bed. "What's on your mind?" she asks tentatively.

I nod at her belly. "Everything okay with the baby?"

Her eyes widen. "Of course. Why do you ask?"

"Well, for starters, you're no bigger than you were five months ago."

Indignation flitters across her features. "I'm lucky, I guess."

"Right, lucky." I thrust my hand through my hair. "Hey, uh, do you have any more sonogram images I can look at?"

She scans the room as if looking for them, but then shakes her head. "No, I don't. But I can get you some."

"How 'bout I just go to your next appointment with you?"

"No," she blurts. "I mean, Dr. Wilde typically just sees me when she's got a few spare minutes in between her patients. There's no way to know when exactly that's going to be."

"Glitter, I want to be at the next appointment," I state firmly while pulling my cell out of my cut and thrusting it at her. "Here. Call and schedule something."

"B-but the office is closed."

Dammit.

"Don't you have Dr. Wilde's home number? Call her directly and set it up."

Glitter tenses for a split-second, but she relaxes so quickly I convince myself I'm making it up.

"Spike, I can't call my boss at home," she says calmly. "That's highly inappropriate."

Heaving a sigh, I shove my phone back into my pocket. "Fine. But I want you to get yourself an actual appointment tomorrow and call me immediately to let me know when it is."

She nods. "Okay. If it's that important to you, I will."

Glitter stands and tries to wrap her arms around me, but I push her away. "Don't mistake this for more than it is," I say gently, not wanting to cause too much distress.

She steps back and crosses her arms over her chest. "Fine. Now can you get outta here so I can shower?"

"Yeah, sure."

I turn and walk toward the door. The motion sensor triggers the door to open, and I pause to look over my shoulder.

"Tomorrow, Glitter. I want that appointment ASAP."

CHAPTER NINETEEN

IVORY

"Have no fear, the Italian food is here!"

My stomach rumbles with Eric's announcement as he stomps into the house with Megan on his heels. I need my friends tonight after my encounter with Aubrey at Dr. Wilde's office. I haven't stopped shaking since I left the parking lot. When I got home, I called Megan to come over, and she called Eric, who in turn called me, asking what I wanted for dinner. I didn't think I'd be able to eat, but if the gurgles in my stomach at the smell of garlic is any indication, I definitely can.

"Gimme, gimme, gimme," I chant while trying to grab the bags.

Eric swats my hands. "Get back you heathen."

"At least let us get it unpacked," Megan chastises.

I stick my bottom lip out, and my chin wobbles of its own accord. "But the baby is hungry now."

"Oh, dear lord, make it stop," Eric says dramatically, handing me a bag. "Here, now, put the lip away."

Thank you hormones.

I smirk and take a seat at the table. Opening the container, I find a huge portion of baked ziti.

Megan hands me a napkin. "You have a little bit of drool right there."

"I do not," I pout, taking the napkin anyway.

"Yes, you do," Eric agrees, opening his container. "You look like a starved little puppy that hasn't eaten all day."

Megan laughs, and I scowl at both of them. This is what I needed tonight. A distraction from the shit-show that has become my life. I still don't know how I got myself into this situation.

You decided to be wild and have a one-night stand with a sexy biker.

After a few bites, the pasta settles like a lead balloon in the pit of my stomach. I move the food around in the container but can't take another bite, so I push away from the table and go into the kitchen. I grab a bottle of wine, a couple of glasses, and a ginger ale.

The fork Megan's holding hovers in front of her mouth when she sees what I'm doing. "Uh oh, what happened?"

"Nothing," I dismiss, uncorking the wine.

"Bullshit, heifer," Eric scolds. "Don't think we didn't notice that you only took a few bites before you stopped eating."

"You sounded off when you called me earlier asking me to come over," Megan adds. "Why do you think I asked Eric to come over too?"

"I figured Eric wanted to see me and the basket-ball I'm growing." I hand them each a glass of wine before settling back in my chair with my ginger ale.

Eric shakes his head. "You know I'm always up for seeing my girlies. And by the way, you're rocking the shit out of the 'bun in the oven' look."

I spit my drink across the table. "Are you serious right now? Bun in the oven?"

"It's better than harboring a future fugitive." Eric holds up his hands in surrender when Megan glares at him. "What? Too soon?"

I laugh humorlessly. "You're not too far off." Tears well in my eyes, and I don't even try to fight them.

"Whoa, Ivory. I-I-I'm sorry," Eric stammers. "I was joking. I didn't mean anything by it. You know my big mouth can't help what comes out of it." Megan opens her mouth to speak, but Eric cuts her off. "I heard it when I said it, heifer."

A giggle escapes before I can stop myself. Hormones are a bitch, I don't care what anyone says.

"I'm okay." I sigh. "My emotions are all over the place. I'm sorry for overreacting."

"No, I was a dick," Eric says. "I'm sorry. Forgive me?"

He drops to one knee and presents me with a giant chunk of garlic bread.

"My hero!" I yell and snatch the carby goodness from him.

He stands and side hugs me before returning to his chair.

"How'd your appointment with Dr. Wilde go?" Megan asks casually.

Chills wrack my body as the memory from today's conversation about the baby slams into me. For a brief moment, I let myself forget.

How could I do that? What kind of mother am I going to be?

Eric grabs my hand and squeezes. "The best damn mother ever."

"Did I say that out loud?" I ask, and they both nod. "Great, I can't even keep my thoughts in my head."

"Ivory, what's going on?" Megan furrows her brows.

I spill my guts and tell them everything that's going on with the baby.

"You know me and Megan will be there for

anything you need," Eric assures. "You won't be alone, and I'm sure the baby will be fine."

"It's a boy," I purr.

"A boy?" they both shout in unison.

"Eek!" Megan squeals.

Eric stands and starts doing the Floss. "I'm gonna be the greatest uncle in history. That boy'll know how to dress to impress."

"There's more," I announce. "I don't know what to do."

Megan tugs me over to the couch, and Eric pops a squat on the floor in front of us. "We're here to help. Tell us," she encourages.

I wrap my arms around my tummy and rock slightly. "I ran into Aubrey."

"Who's Aubrey?" Eric asks, confused.

I realize I never told them what I found out at my initial prenatal appointment. I explain who Aubrey is and the first conversation we had.

"No fucking way!" Megan snaps. "He had a woman at home and then had the audacity to sleep with you? And now you're both knocked up?"

"Yep," I say, popping the 'p.' "That's not all, though. After I found out that the baby has to have surgery, I decided I can't keep this secret from Spike. No matter how much I despise him, he has a right to know. If Spike still doesn't want anything to do with us, then that's on him."

"Exactly," Eric agrees.

"I'm sensing a but coming," Megan hedges.

"You'd be right," I confirm. "I wanted to be honest and not have it look like I'm creeping behind Aubrey's back." I take a deep breath before continuing. "I asked her to meet me outside as I was leaving. I told her what Dr. Wilde said and emphasized that I don't want Spike in any way, shape, or form. But he does have a right to know what's happening with his son. She went ballistic. Basically, she thinks that I'm a homewrecker and that I can't prove the baby is Spike's."

"Yes, you ca—"

"No, I can't. Not without a paternity test," I tell them. "Aubrey's right. It's her word against mine. She also said that the club takes lying very seriously, and that if I pursue this, I'll end up dead before I even give birth.

Both Megan and Eric flinch, but neither of them speaks for a few minutes.

Eric breaks the silence first. "I don't believe that for one goddamn minute. I've been to Purgatory without you all and have seen firsthand what happens. Not once have I seen one of them step out when their lady wasn't around. And believe me, many women try to get in their pants."

"Maybe Spike meets his side pieces discreetly," I counter.

"Nope," Eric argues. "RaRa and I talked about it. He told me that they'd rather cut out their own heart and have their dicks ripped off than hurt their old ladies. I didn't want to say anything because I know you have strong feelings about not telling Spike, but I've never seen him with anyone at the bar. All the other old ladies are always there with their men, but Spike… He's always alone."

"Ivory," Megan says softly. "It's possible that Aubrey is lying to keep you away. From what you told us, she always goes on the defense with *you*. If I were Aubrey, I'd drag your ass to Purgatory and make him admit to everyone what a lying, cheating asshole he is."

"Not everyone has your decorum," Eric teases.

"You know what I mean," she hisses. "He drove over here that day to talk to you, *and* he pleaded for you to hear him out. Does that sound like a man who wouldn't care about his unborn son?"

"Jokes aside, I agree with Megan. You need to talk to him," Eric encourages. "We can be there with you if you want. You don't have to face him alone."

Now that Megan's pointed that out, it does seem unlikely, but it doesn't ward off the fear.

"I'll think about it." I lie.

Megan and Eric help me clean up the mess from dinner and head out.

"Call me if you need us," Megan demands.

"I will," I promise.

"Don't think I don't know you're lying about talking to Spike," Eric chastises. "If I thought for one minute you and the baby would be in danger, I'd pack you up and get you the hell out of here. Something isn't adding up, and until you talk to him, you're never gonna know the truth, and neither will he."

"Thanks for the food and listening." I kiss them both on the cheek.

"We're here for you, night or day," Megan says, leading Eric to her car.

I give a small wave before closing the door and locking it tight. After crawling into bed, I let Eric's words replay over and over in my head about what he's observed at Purgatory.

Spike deserves to know. I'll make it clear that I don't want a relationship with him or want to interfere in his life with Aubrey, but I have to tell him. He just has a right to know he has a son, and that said son needs surgery.

I can only pray I'm making the right decision.

Time to prove what kind of man you are, Spike.

CHAPTER TWENTY

SPIKE

"THAT'LL BE ONE SEVENTEEN FIFTY-TWO."

I hand my card to the cashier and wait while she runs the transaction through. As soon as she hands it back, I return it to my wallet and grab the bag with my purchase.

"Have a good one," I say as I walk out of the store.

I wasn't planning on leaving Sinful Wheels at all today, but I broke one of my tools when I threw it at the wall for not cooperating and needed to replace it immediately. Besides, the ride to the store gave me a chance to clear my head and calm down.

As I'm walking to my bike, I pull out my cell to text Knuckles, who's holding down the fort at the shop while I'm gone. Before I can hit send, my phone is knocked out of my hand when someone bumps into me. I lift my head and open my mouth to give the fucker an earful but quickly freeze.

"Ivory."

She immediately puts the bag she's carrying in front of her like a barrier. "Spike, I, uh…"

My eyes drop to the logo of a baby in a cradle on the bag, and my hackles rise. "Doing some shopping?"

She lowers her head for a moment before squaring her shoulders, leveling her dark eyes on mine, and dropping the bag to the ground next to her.

"You could say that," she says, defiance in her tone.

Shock kicks me in the gut worse than any horse ever could. "You're pregnant."

"I am."

"Wow, um… How far along are you?"

Ivory pulls her brows together. "About as far along as Aubrey," she hisses.

"Aubrey?"

She huffs out a breath and picks up her bag. "Yeah, you know… your baby mama."

"Glitter?" I ask. "How do you know Glitter?"

"Who's Glitter?"

I bend to pick up my phone and shove it in my cut which gives me a moment to collect my thoughts. Running into Ivory was not on my to-do list for the day, not to mention finding out that she's pregnant *and* knows Glitter.

"Can we start over?" I ask when I straighten.

"Where exactly?" she sasses. "Do you wanna go all the way back to before that dare of yours, or are you talking about just the last few minutes?"

I arch a brow. "Whichever one gets you to settle down and actually talk to me."

For a split-second I worry she'll turn around and storm in the opposite direction, but she surprises me when she nods curtly.

"I *am* kinda hungry," she admits. "There's a diner just up the street where I was gonna grab a quick bite to eat. You can join me if you want."

Ivory steps around me to walk toward the restaurant, leaving me to follow. And shamelessly, I do.

"Just the two of you?" the hostess asks when we enter.

"Yes," I confirm. "And if you've got a booth near the back, that'd be great."

"Picky much," Ivory mutters.

"As a matter of fact," I begin as the hostess leads us through the diner. "Yes, I am. I like to be able to see the entire restaurant. Makes it easier to see any threats before trouble happens."

We slide into the booth, and the hostess tosses the menus onto the table before walking away.

"You expecting trouble?" Ivory asks.

"Always."

I don't bother looking at the menu, but I remain silent while Ivory peruses her options. After the waitress comes to take our order, we're finally alone.

"So, pregnant, huh?"

That's the best you can do, idiot?

"Yep."

"And you're what… about five months along?"

"Same as Aubrey."

"That bothers you," I say dryly. "Why?"

"Because that means you slept with me while you weren't exactly free to do so."

"Wait a minute…" I shake my head. "I was, and still am, completely *free*, as you put it, to fuck whoever the hell I want."

"And that's all I was to you… a good fuck." Tears glisten in her eyes, and she can't stop them from spilling over. "Glad to know where I stand."

"I'm sorry, Ivory," I begin. "But, clearly, you've found someone else so what's it matter?"

"It matt—"

"Here ya go," the waitress says as she slides our plates onto the table. "I'll be right back with your drinks."

"Excuse me," Ivory mumbles and slips out of the booth to rush to the bathroom.

By the time she returns, our drinks have been delivered, and I'm halfway through my burger.

"This was a mistake," she says when she sits.

"Just eat," I instruct, no heat in my tone. "I'm sure the baby's hungry."

Ivory chuckles, genuine happiness shining through for the first time since we bumped into each other. "That he is."

"He?"

Her head whips up, and her eyes widen. "Uh, yeah. I'm having a boy."

How is it that I don't even know what Glitter's having?

"Congrats."

She takes a deep breath. "You, too."

"Oh, we don't know what we're having yet."

"With Aubrey, maybe. But you *are* gonna have a son."

"I don't see how you could poss—"

"You really haven't figured it out, have you?"

Stiffening, I frown. "Figured what out?"

"Hunter, c'mon," she cajoles, rubbing her round belly. "We hooked up a little over five months ago, and I'm pregnant. I haven't slept with anyone other than you in almost a year. I'm sure even you can put two and two together."

Her words register, and everything clicks into

place. "It's mine," I say, not meaning for it to come out as a statement.

"He is."

"You're pregnant with my baby?"

"Yes, Hunter, I am."

"You keep calling me Hunter. Why?"

Ivory shrugs. "When I'm talking to the father of my child, I'm gonna use his real name."

"Okay, yeah, I'm good with that." As the news settles, anger surfaces. "Were you ever gonna tell me?"

"That I'm pregnant?"

The more I think about it, the more enraged I become. "No, that you're a woman," I snap. "Yes, that you're pregnant."

"I wan—"

"Never mind," I bite out. "I forgot who I was talking to."

"What the hell's that supposed to mean?"

"You're the same chick who ran out on me the morning after because you were too ashamed to have slept with a biker." I scoot out of the booth and stand. Yanking my wallet out of my back pocket, I grab two twenties and toss them on the table. "If you think for one second that you're gonna keep my son from me, think again."

And with that, I storm out of the diner, ignoring the stares of other patrons.

It's not lost on me that I didn't for one second question whether or not Ivory was telling the truth about the baby being mine. There's just something about her that screams *honesty*. But then I remember that she lied about one pretty big thing.

What the fuck am I gonna do now?

CHAPTER TWENTY-ONE
IVORY

*W*HAT JUST HAPPENED?

Shock fills me as I watch Spike storm down the sidewalk and hop on his bike. He never even glances my way as he speeds off. I take a moment and gather myself, thankful that he wanted to sit at the back because no one can see my tear-stricken face. I pull my compact out of my purse and gently blot powder around my eyes to dull the run in my mascara.

I should've worn the waterproof kind. Nothing I can do about it now. Lesson for next time…

There won't be a next time. Never again will I let this man hurt me.

The bell above the deli door rings again, and laughter fills the air. I'm not in the mood to watch happy-go-lucky people go about their business when my life is falling apart, especially after the father of my child walked out on me.

I push away from the table and turn, only to see a familiar face in front of me.

"Hey, Ivory!" Skye greets excitedly. "How've you…" Her voice trails off as her eyes roam over my face and body. "Are you okay?"

"Yeah," I answer quickly, brushing at the lingering tears. "Sorry, I need to go. Nice to see you again."

I grab my purse when another woman steps up beside Skye. "Who's this, Skye?" she asks.

"Wait, are you pregnant?" Skye inquires, ignoring the other woman completely and staring at my protruding belly.

I lower my bag in front of my stomach in a poor attempt to conceal the pregnancy. "I'm sorry, Skye," I apologize. "I'm in a hurry. I'll see you around." I scootch around the other woman and head for the door.

"Wait," Skye calls. I halt a few paces from the door. "Please, stay and talk to me."

I hang my head and weigh my options.

This could be a trap that Aubrey set up, or Spike could've called them to deal with me since Aubrey is probably at work. Don't be stupid, it's broad daylight in a public place. They can't do anything here.

I slowly walk back toward the table and sit across from Skye.

"I'm Cece," the beautiful woman says. She reaches her hand over, and I shake it.

"Ivory," I reply.

"Okay, woman. Spill," Skye demands. "I can tell you've been crying, and hell, it doesn't take a rocket scientist to see you're pregnant."

"There's nothing to tell," I mumble, tears welling in my eyes again. *Damn hormones.* I bite the inside of my cheek to keep them from tumbling over.

"Bullshit," Skye spits out.

"Skye, enough," Cece chastises. "It's okay. We just want to help. I know you don't know me, but obviously, you know who Skye is. I can tell she considers you a friend. She's overly protective, and when she sees a friend hurting, she goes all mama bear."

"Her opinion of me is about to change then… *if* she considers me a friend," I say cryptically. "Do you remember that afternoon I came to Purgatory to find Spike?"

Skye nods, and realization dawns in her eyes. "Did you know you were pregnant?"

"Yes," I admit. "I was looking for him so I could tell him."

"I gave him your number," she confirms. "Did he not call?"

"No, he called." I sigh. "He called and was a royal

dick and said some shit that pissed me off. I hung up on him before I could tell him."

"Lord save us from hot-headed, bruised ego alpha men," Cece says.

Skye giggles. "Unfortunately, I don't think that'll ever change. You, however, get to deal with the worst alpha."

"Not true!" Cece throws a napkin at her. "Malice is way worse. I feel bad for Apple. Soul's a puppy dog compared to that man's temper."

"You're right." Skye holds up her hands in surrender. "I wouldn't let Soul hear you call him a puppy dog, though."

"Why not?" Cece wiggles her brows. "The wall sex is worth it. What a punishment!"

"You're incorrigible." Skye focuses her attention back on me. "Spike went to see you that night."

"He did," I confirm, my head spinning from their back-and-forth banter. "It never came up. After I hung up on him, I decided that I would raise the baby myself. In my defense," I rush to continue. "I was a hormonal mess, and Spike proved to me exactly what kind of man he is when he was screaming at me. Plus, I was trying to come to terms that I got pregnant after a one-night stand with a biker. I wasn't thinking clearly."

Cece's eyes soften. "I get it. I was a hot mess the

entire time I was pregnant with my daughter. It's hard to navigate around all those feelings."

My lip curves up slightly. "Yeah, it's been a nightmare. A roller coaster of feelings. I never know when I'm going to laugh, cry, or pee my pants."

Cece's laughter echoes in the restaurant. "Girl, that won't go away. Trust me."

"Great," I pout. "It's bad enough I'm carrying a basketball, and my back is constantly sore. Now I have to worry about pissing myself for the rest of my life."

"Yep!"

"Let's go back a minute," Skye interrupts. "Spike is the father, right?"

I nod. "I went to my first appointment a couple of weeks later and heard the baby's heartbeat. I fell in love instantly with Peanut." I glance down and rub my tummy. "I decided it wasn't right to keep this secret from Spike and that I was being unfair."

"Hold on," Cece interjects. "Spike still doesn't know."

"I told him today," I admit.

"Why didn't you tell him earlier?" Skye asks, her eyes narrowing.

I take a deep breath. "His old lady threatened me."

Skye's eyes dart to Cece, and both of their mouths drop open.

What the hell is going on? I should've kept my fucking mouth shut.

"I should go," I rise to my feet. "It was good seeing you again. I won't cause the club any trouble. You'll never see or hear from me again. Tell Spike I'll forget he exists."

Cece is the first one to break the silence and grabs my arm. "Don't go," she pleads. "We're just shocked." Cece and Skye share a look. "Did you say Spike's old lady threatened you?"

"Look, I-I-I don't want any problems," I stutter, my voice wobbling. "I'll disappear with the ba——"

"Spike doesn't have an old lady," Skye says gently.

I shake my head in denial. "Yes, he does. She works at my OB's office. She knew his legal name, things about the club… This doesn't make sense."

It does make sense, though, the more I think about everything that's happened. If Megan is right, then Aubrey's been filling my head with lies to keep me away from Spike, but why? It doesn't matter in the grand scheme of things since she's also pregnant with his child.

"What's her name?" Cece prods.

"Aubrey," I answer.

"Aubrey?" Cece taps her chin. "I don't know anyone named Aubrey."

"Did you say she works at your doctor's office?" Skye inquires.

"Yeah, she's a receptionist there," I add.

"Fucking Glitter," Skye hisses. "That stupid fucking cunt. I knew she was bad news."

"Spike mentioned Glitter, too," I say, confused. "Who the hell is she?"

"Glitter is Aubrey," Cece explains. "Glitter is a club bunny." My brows furrow in confusion. "Club bunnies are there to service the uncommitted men, the ones without an old lady. When our men commit, they *do not* cheat. I won't lie to you. Spike has been with her, but they are *not* together. She's *not* his old lady. In fact, he hasn't been with her since he met you."

I fidget in my seat. "There's more."

"More?" Cece asks incredulously.

I close my eyes and take a deep breath. "After Aubrey told me she was Spike's old lady and that she was also pregnant, I vowed to her I wouldn't tell Spike about my baby. Things changed when I went in for my ultrasound last week." I pause. Skye squeezes my hand, giving me the courage to continue. "The baby has to have an emergency surgery when he's born because he has a diaphragmatic hernia. It can be life-threatening if not treated immediately after birth."

Cece gasps. "Omigod. Are you okay? Is the baby okay?"

"I'm okay, he's okay," I assure them both. "I really wanted Spike to know that he was going to have a son and that he was going to need surgery. I swear I wasn't trying to start drama with Aubrey."

"We know. What happened next?"

I tell them everything from how I asked Aubrey to meet me outside after my appointment and how I told her what's wrong with the baby. I end the story with how she threatened me with the club and that if I told anyone, it would be her word against mine since she was an old lady and I'm just a home-wrecking slut.

"It didn't help that she told me I'd end up with a bullet in me before my son was ever born," I tack on.

"She said what?" Cece sneers. "Glitter told you... The club would kill you and your unborn child if you told Spike you were pregnant?"

I slump back against the cushioned booth, extremely exhausted from all the revelations. All I can do is nod.

"Come on." Skye stands and pulls me to my feet. "We need to go to the club and talk to Spike."

That knocks me out of my stupor. "No… no… I can't. Please don't make me," I beg. "You all might believe me, but I can't take a chance with my safety. I have to think about my baby."

"Spike deserves to know," Skye counters.

"He does," I say softly. "And I would've told him if he hadn't yelled at me and stormed out. Obviously he doesn't care one way or another about us. Please, just… let it go."

Skye juts her chin out in annoyance. "I can't believe that asshole left you here. I'm gonna kill him."

"It's not worth it." I gather my things. "We'll be okay. I have great friends who'll be there for us. Spike can focus on Aubrey's baby. He deserved to know, and now he does. Spike made his choice when he turned his back on me and walked away."

"Come on, Ivory," Cece begs. "Give him another chance. There has to be more we don't know about. This doesn't sound like Spike at all."

"I can't keep doing this," I cry. "I have to think about my son. *He* is my priority. You might know Spike better than I do, but he has shown his true colors more than once to me. If you really want to help me, keep him and Aubrey away from me."

I rush out of the diner before they can stop me again. Spike knows he has another child coming into this world. I can sleep at night knowing I'm no longer keeping this secret from him.

That doesn't mean I have to let him into our lives. Aubrey or Glitter or whatever her name is, got her wish. She can keep Spike all to herself.

CHAPTER TWENTY-TWO

SPIKE

"You've been down here for hours."

I grab the punching bag to stop it from swinging as I shift my gaze to the wall-sized mirror at Abyss's reflection. As soon as I left the diner, I returned to Sinful Wheels and told Knuckles that I was taking the rest of the day off. Then I came home and dove into working out my rage in the gym.

"So."

"So, it's not like you," he counters. "Not to mention that it's the middle of the workday."

Slowly, I turn around to face my brother. For the most part, Abyss has remained fairly quiet about my situation with Glitter, and for some reason, that makes me want to open up to him about Ivory.

"Ya got a few minutes?" I ask.

He nods and strides to the bench and sits. Before I join him, I pace for a few minutes in an attempt to put my thoughts in order. Unfortunately, pacing doesn't help one iota, so I decide to jump right in.

"Ivory's pregnant."

"Ivory? The chick who left the morning after?"

"One and the same."

"Okay. And this has you in knots because…"

"I'm the father."

"She told you that?"

"Yes."

"And you believe her?" he counters. "She wouldn't be the first girl to try and trap a biker with a bogus pregnancy."

Instant fury bubbles in my gut, and I lunge at him. I shove him off the bench, and when he hits the floor, he grunts as he stares at me incredulously.

"She's not lying," I snarl.

"Right. Okay." He holds a hand out for me to help him to his feet. As soon as he's upright, he continues. "What about Glitter?"

I huff out a breath. "What about her?"

"Don't be stupid. You know exactly what I'm asking about."

"She still insists she's pregnant. But…" I run both hands through my hair. "Fucking hell, I don't know what to think."

"What does your gu—"

"There you are!"

Abyss and I whirl toward the door where Skye and Cece are barreling over the threshold with their arms crossed over their chests.

"We're in the middle of so—"

"I don't care if you're preparing for a visit from the Pope himself," Cece snaps, closing the distance between us. "How dare you treat Ivory the way you have."

"Pretty sure this is the last place the Pope would wanna be," I say, trying to make a joke, but it falls on deaf ears.

"You left her in that diner, sobbing her heart out," Skye accuses.

"And on that note, I'm outta here." Abyss strides out of the room, leaving me to deal with the old ladies.

"She lied to me," I tell them. "She's pregnant with my son, and she li—"

"Give me a break, Spike," Cece seethes. "She didn't want to keep anything from you, but she didn't have a choice."

"There's always a choice."

"Not when a skanky bitch threatens to have her and her unborn child killed by the club for stealing..." Skye lifts her hands and makes air quotes. "... 'her man'."

"What are you talking about?" I ask.

"She's talking about Glitter," Cece clarifies. "Fucking bitch told Ivory that you and she are an item, and that Ivory better stay away or else."

Rage like I've never felt runs through my veins like lava. "She did what?" I growl.

"You heard me. Ivory wanted to tell you, but she was scared for her life and the life of *your* son."

"I'll kill her."

I stomp past them toward the door, but Cece grabs my arm and halts me in my tracks.

"Soul's already called church," she informs me, and when I narrow my eyes in confusion, she continues. "I filled him in as soon as I got here. He said he was calling church and to tell you to get your ass in there."

My expression softens. "Thanks, Cece."

I rush out of the gym, through the hall and common room, and come to a stop outside the door to the room where church is held. Possum comes from the other direction and stops next to me.

"We gonna stand here all day or go in?"

I take a deep breath. "Go in."

"Then get a move on."

We're the last two in the room, and judging by the looks on everyone's faces, Soul started without us.

"Two babies," Frenzy comments. "Sucks to be you."

"Don't let Heather hear you say that," Rogue states, referring to Frenzy's old lady.

"Have a seat, and we'll get started," Malice instructs.

Once Possum and I are in our chairs, Soul calls the meeting to order.

"I'll let you fill them in," Prez says.

"Not sure I know any more than you do," I admit. "But what I do know is bad enough."

"Care to share with the class?" Thorn asks sarcastically.

"The short version is that Glitter threatened Ivory," I explain. "Bitch told her that if she told me she was pregnant, the club would retaliate by offing her and the baby."

Grim shoots to his feet and lifts his hands. "You're not fucking serious."

"Deadly," I confirm. "No pun intended."

"Why the hell would she do that?" Abyss asks.

"Apparently, she told Ivory that she's my old lady." I shrug. "Staking her claim, I guess. But it doesn't matter *why* she did it, just that she did."

"I don't know about anyone else, but I wanna get Glitter in here and get some answers," Rogue states. "I know that's typically reserved for the Confessional, but she's pregnant, so…"

"About that…" I run my fingers through my

already disheveled hair. "I'm not sure she actually is pregnant. She was all sketchy when I asked to go to her next doctor's appointment."

"Well, until we know for sure, we question her here," Soul says. "Possum, go get her."

"You got it," Possum says as he rises and leaves the room.

It's not two minutes later, and he practically drags her in behind him. He leads her to an empty chair and pushes down on her shoulders to force her to sit.

"Uh, what's this all about?" Glitter asks nervously. She tries to stand, but Possum remains behind her and doesn't let her move.

Soul and I exchange a look, and he nods, silently giving me permission to do the questioning. I shift my eyes to Glitter and scowl.

"Make that appointment yet?" I ask, lulling her into a false sense of security.

"Oh, um... the thing is... I tr—"

"Cut the shit," I snap, pounding my fists on the table, causing her to jump. "Are you even pregnant?"

Her hands immediately go to her still-flat stomach as she hesitates. "Of... Of course, I am."

"You're what? Five months along?" Soul asks.

"'Bout that."

"Damn. That sucks," Prez says.

"Why do you say that?" Glitter asks.

"Well, I'm sure your doctor started your weekly injections of placenta booster."

What?

"Oh, yeah." Glitter nods enthusiastically. "She got me going on those a few weeks ago."

Soul shoves his chair back and stomps around the table to grab her by the hair and yank her to her feet. "You fucking bitch," he seethes. "You're not pregnant."

Glitter tries to free herself from his grip but fails. "I am pregnant," she cries.

"There's no such thing as placenta booster injections," Abyss informs her.

Instantly, Glitter slumps in Soul's grasp. "Oh."

"Time to fess up, you stupid bitch," I snap. "You're not pregnant, are you?"

She crosses her arms over her chest defiantly. "No. I'm not pregnant. Satisfied?"

"Not even the tiniest fucking bit." I stand and lean with my palms on the table. "You threatened Ivory," I say, not even bothering to form the words into a question.

Her eyes widen. "She was gonna steal you from me!"

"I don't belong to you!" I shout and swing my hands back and forth between us. "You and me... there is nothing there."

"But there could be," she whines.

"No, there couldn't. I don't even like you, much less like you enough to pursue a relationship."

"But you had sex with me!" she shrieks.

"Newsflash, cunt," Malice interjects. "You're a club bunny which makes your sole purpose here to fuck any of us who are unattached. Sex is kinda the only thing in the job description."

"I don't believe this," Glitter complains. "I've done nothing wrong."

"The fact that you think that, shows us just how beyond insane you are," Thorn states.

"Malice, get her the fuck outta here," Soul demands. "Grab Mark and any old lady who's here and take them all downstairs. Let the old ladies dole out punishment in the Confessional while you and Mark stand guard in case they need you. Then kick her sorry ass off the property."

"You're gonna let the women handle her?" I ask, annoyed that I'm not able to do it.

"I am," he confirms. "I want her punished, not dead." He shifts his stare to Glitter. "At least, not yet. You show your face around here again or do anything to cause harm to a single person I give a damn about, and I'll let the brothers kill you. Got it?"

Glitter nods, seemingly resigned to her fate.

Malice stands and stalks in her direction. As soon as he has her out of the room, all focus turns to Soul.

"Church is dismissed," he says before leveling his gaze on me. "I suggest you talk to Ivory, and the sooner, the better. I don't want her thinking she's in danger from us."

"Oh, I plan to," I assure him.

Grim pounds on the table until we all glance at him. He lifts his hands and smirks. "I lost count of how many of you owe fifty bucks."

"Jesus," Soul mutters. "Fine. We'll each pay the fifty bucks, and the money can be pooled for a baby gift for Ivory. That okay with you, ya big oaf?"

Grim nods. "Yep."

"Get the hell outta my sight, all of you," Soul demands.

The room empties out quickly, and I make my way to my room to shower before going to see Ivory. We need to have a long talk, and it can't wait.

CHAPTER TWENTY-THREE

GLITTER

"If you ever step foot in Boulder City again, we'll make you disappear *permanently*. Consider this your only warning."

I lift my chin in acknowledgment but don't respond to Malice's threat. Mark sneers at me as he tosses my things at my feet. They stand side by side with their arms crossed, watching my every movement. Wrapping my arm around my waist, I wince as I bend over to grab my purse and the small bag of my belongings.

I hobble to my car, groaning as I climb inside and start the engine. I pull out of my spot and leave the clubhouse behind. The garage door closes with finality as I exit the side of the mountain.

Glancing in the rearview mirror, I'm not surprised at the face looking back at me. One eye is completely swollen shut, blood drips from my nose, and bruises mar the side of my face. It hurts to take a deep breath. Luckily for them, I don't think anything is broken.

They fucking beat me!

They could've killed my baby. Spike only agreed with Soul and the others because he was afraid they'd kick him out of the club. He loves me, I know he does. This is all that stupid bitch's fault. Ivory's a fucking liar who turned the entire club against me.

They have no idea what I'm capable of.

"I'll fucking show them." I cradle my stomach as I drive. "Don't worry, Daddy will see how much we love him. That homewrecking cunt will be on the receiving end next time. I'll be welcomed back with open arms, and everyone will be so consumed with guilt for the pain they caused me."

I should go to the police and have them tear apart the clubhouse.

But I can't. This is just a test. It has to be. It's a test of loyalty. They want me to prove that I'm tough enough to handle being a biker's old lady.

Spike knows Ivory's too soft for this life. I'll show them how tough I can be.

I hit the highway with a plan formulating.

"I'll fucking show them all."

CHAPTER TWENTY-FOUR

IVORY

"Ivory, some big mean-looking guy is at the counter looking for you."

My head snaps up to see Jackie standing in the doorway. Megan unlocks the side drawer in her desk and pulls out her gun, clicking off the safety. We both know how to shoot and handle guns, and Megan even has her concealed carry permit. She's been begging me to get mine, but I always refuse. I kinda wish I didn't, but I never thought I'd need a weapon at work.

Megan stands. "What's he look like?"

"Shoulder-length dirty blonde hair, beard, and tattoos and muscles everywhere," Jackie informs us, her eyes wide. "Jeremy's threatening to call the cops if he doesn't leave. I came back here to warn you. He doesn't look like someone who should be messed with."

"I told Skye to leave it alone," I mumble, rising to my feet. "I'll take care of it."

"You sure, Ivory?" Jackie asks. "Jeremy was handling it."

Megan smirks, putting her gun away. "I don't think cops would scare Spike away."

"I'll handle him." I gesture to the chair in the corner. "Take a break for a few minutes."

"Do you want me to come with you?" Megan asks.

I wave her off. "No, I need to deal with this once and for all."

"Yell if you need me," she calls.

Spike and Jeremy are in a standoff when I come around the corner into the waiting area.

"Look, pal, I don't know who you are, but you have five seconds to leave before I call the cops," Jeremy states firmly. "There's no one named Ivory here."

Spike points to the wall. "Then why the fuck is there a picture of her right there?"

"She… uh… that's a friend of the owner," Jeremy stutters.

Spike crosses his arms, making his muscles bulge. His Henley tightens around his arms. I have to give Jeremy credit, he's not backing down. My ninja skills must not be up to par because both of their heads jerk in my direction.

"Not here, huh?" Spike says smugly.

Jeremy puffs out his chest. "You want her, you'll have to go through me."

I rush forward as fast as my pregnancy allows, putting myself between them. The last thing I need is Jeremy getting beat to a bloody pulp. Laying my hand on Jeremy's chest, I gently push him back.

"I got this, Jeremy," I say. "Why don't you go back with Megan and Jackie?"

"I'll stand over there." He jerks his chin to the counter. "I won't leave you out here alone."

"I'm not gonna fucking hurt her," Spike roars. "For fuck's sake, she's carrying m—"

"Outside!" I scream, poking Spike in the chest. "Right now!"

I glance over my shoulder when I hear feet shuffling behind me. Megan and Jackie head toward us. but I mouth, *'I'm okay' before* following Spike out the door. Once we're outside, I see all of them standing by the counter to watch the soap opera unfolding.

Great. My life's become a Jerry Springer episode. Now we just need the envelope... You are the father!

"What're you doing here, Spike?" I question. "More importantly, how'd you find me?"

Spike glares at the window behind me. "We need to talk."

"The time for talking was yesterday when I told you I was pregnant with your son."

"Seriously, Ivory? You owe me this much."

Laughter bubbles up and escapes. The tension from the past few months breaks free, and I can't stop. I'm sure I look hysterical. And my ribs hurt from laughing so hard.

"I-I-I owe you? That's rich." I gasp for breath and straighten my spine as I narrow my eyes, all traces of humor gone. "I owe you fucking *nothing*. Every time I try talking to you, you throw a goddamn hissy fit and disappear. Fuck you, Spike. Get the hell outta here before Jeremy calls the police, or Megan shoots your ass. At this point, I'm fine with either of those outcomes."

I spin on my heel to head back inside when Spike grabs my bicep.

"Let. Me. Go," I say with deadly calm and turn around slowly to face him.

He immediately drops my arm. "Please, Ivory." Spike rubs his hand over his face. "I know I don't deserve it. I've been a complete asshole, but please give me one more chance to make this right."

I stare at him and see hurt, anger, and uncertainty flash across his face.

"Fine, but not here," I concede. "I don't need to put on a show for my coworkers."

"I can meet you at you—"

"No. Somewhere public."

"How about Dob's Diner in an hour?" he suggests.

"I'll be there," I promise. "This is the last time, Spike. I'm not doing this anymore with you. I have *our* son to think about. You might not give a damn, but I sure as hell do."

Spike rears back as if I slapped him. He doesn't respond but jerks his chin and swings his leg over his bike. The ground rumbles under my feet as he peels out of our parking lot.

God, don't make me regret this.

I go back inside, ignoring all the faces staring intently at me, and make my way to the office. Megan follows, shutting the door behind her.

I focus on my computer screen, but I can feel her eyes burning into my skull.

"Just say it," I spit out.

"You're gonna meet him, aren't you?" she says with no judgment.

"I told him we could talk. In public," I stress.

"Uh-huh," she mocks. "Afraid to be alone with him? You do realize you can't get any more pregnant, right?"

I throw a pen at her. "I don't *want* him, Megan."

"Okay," she draws out. "You can lie to me, but don't lie to yourself."

I flinch. "How can you say that after everything he's put me through?"

A small smile plays on her lips. "Babe, think about it. You're both to blame for this situation." I open my mouth to argue, but she continues before I can get a word out. "Yes, you're pregnant and hormonal, but girl, you two have chemistry. That night at Purgatory when you danced with him, I knew then that something electric was brewing between you both. You're stubborn when you're pissed off. I get that. And you have every right to be with all that's happened, but honey, so does he. You kept this secret at first out of anger, which has had a snowball effect, and after everything that's happened, he still wants to talk to you."

I close my mouth as her words sink in. Megan's right, but I'll never admit it to her because her head will get bigger than it already is. If I told Spike about the baby the night he came to my house, this might have all been avoided.

Or maybe not because Aubrey *is still a factor.*

"I'll be back later." I give Megan a quick hug.

"Good luck," she calls out to me as I'm rushing out of the building.

I walk into Dob's Diner an hour later and spot Spike in a booth. My mouth salivates as the smell of greasy fries hits my nose. The waitress stops at our table after I slide in across from Spike.

She's holding a pad of paper and a pen. "What can I get you?"

"Double cheeseburger, extra fries, side salad with ranch dressing, double chocolate shake, and an iced tea, please."

Spike snickers as the waitress writes down my order before she asks him what he wants. "Same thing, but no salad or shake."

"No problem, I'll bring your drinks out shortly," she says.

After she walks away, we stare at each other for a moment before either of us speaks.

"I'm sorry," we both say at the same time.

"I'll go first," I offer, and he waves for me to continue. "I had every intention of telling you I was pregnant the night Skye gave you my number, but when you called... I couldn't deal with your hatred and the fact that you called me an uptight bitch. When you showed up at my house later, I was so pissed at you for talking to me like I was dirt. I didn't feel you deserved to know."

"Ivory, I..."

"Let me finish, please," I plead. "I went for my

first ultrasound and saw the baby's heartbeat, and all I could think about was him and how unfair it was for me to keep this from you. I vowed right then and there to make it right. Aubrey or Glitter, whoever she is, followed me and told me lies about you being her old man. Then Skye and Cece told me you don't have an old lady... is that true?"

"That's true," he verifies. "I'm not in a committed relationship. If I were, I never would've slept with you, I swear."

"That's what they said," I admit. "After I found out the baby needs surgery after he's born, the guilt ate at me, and even though I promised Aubrey I'd never tell you, I knew you had a right to know."

Spike's mouth tightens. "That when she threatened to have you fucking killed?"

I gulp. "Yes. Megan and Eric made me realize that it could all be an elaborate lie fabricated to keep you to herself. I was going to call you that day, but we ran into each other while I was running errands."

"How's the baby?"

I tell him everything Dr. Wilde explained to me, and what would happen after he was born and how long he would be in the NICU after. I don't gloss over any details.

Neither of us speak as our waitress brings us our beverages. I take a long pull of the shake and groan.

Chocolate is better than sex!

"I don't know about that," Spike counters. "I happen to think sex is pretty fucking spectacular."

My cheeks warm. "Said that out loud, didn't I?"

"Yep," he says. "My turn?" I nod and take another sip. "I'm sorry for being such a dick and not being someone you could turn to." He rubs the back of his neck. "I'll be honest, I don't know what to believe, Ivory. I look at you and see nothing but sincerity, but Glitter lied to me about being pregnant with my kid, and here you are saying you're pregnant with my kid, too."

"Aubrey's baby isn't yours?" I ask, shocked.

"She's not pregnant at all," he snips. "Fucking lied to trap me."

I reach across the table and squeeze his hand. "I'm so sorry, Spike. That's unforgivable. No one should ever play with someone's emotions like that." I pause as he stares into my eyes. "I know you have no reason to believe me, but I'll consent to a paternity test after my son is born. We can do it once he's healed from his surgery to prove to you that he's yours."

"Our son," he states firmly.

"Our son," I agree.

The waitress delivers our food, and we eat in

comfortable silence. Spike's eyes widen in shock when I finish everything in front of me.

"Damn woman," he says, pulling out his wallet. "You could put all my brothers to shame."

"Hey, I'm eating for two," I whine.

Spike stands and pulls me out of the booth. "Now what do we do?"

"I have a doctor's appointment tomorrow. Dr. Wilde is going to do another ultrasound." I play with the hem of my shirt, not wanting to meet his gaze. "You can come with me if you want, but I'll warn you, Aubrey works there."

He tips my chin up. "We don't have to worry about her," he assures me. "I want to go with you."

"Okay," I say breathlessly. Suddenly, I don't really feel like being alone. "Do you, uh, wanna come back to stay at my house?"

The corners of his mouth curve up. "Really?"

I smack his chest. "Not for sex, perv. It's an early appointment, and I don't feel like being alone after rehashing all of this stuff." I shrug nonchalantly. "You'll sleep in the spare room, of course."

"Of course," he mocks but not unkindly. "Sure, I'll stay." He tugs me into his chest. "Someday babe, you'll be screaming my name again," he promises.

I wink. "I know. It'll be in the delivery room when I'm cussing and damning you to hell."

Spike throws his head back and laughs.

For the first time in months, things are bright.

I hope, for our son's sake, Spike will be the dad he'll need.

CHAPTER TWENTY-FIVE

SPIKE

One month later...

"Is she coming out for breakfast?"

I pour myself a cup of coffee before moving to the table in the kitchen where Abyss has a feast spread out. He's been making huge meals every morning since Ivory started staying here. She made the mistake of complaining that she was starving one day, and he's made it his personal mission to make sure that's never the case again.

"Nah. She's still sleeping."

"Go wake her up," Abyss orders. "She needs to eat."

"Bro, I know. I won't let her starve, I promise,"

"Fine," he huffs and points at me with a spatula. "See that you don't."

Ivory's been staying at the clubhouse for a few weeks now, and we've settled into a comfortable routine. I love having her here where I can keep an eye on her. Having her close has also given us the opportunity to really get to know each other and build a relationship.

More and more, I find myself thinking about how much I want her in my life. Her *and* our son. Before meeting Ivory at Purgatory, I'd started to realize I was missing something in my life, but that thought hasn't crossed my mind since. She's filled all the voids in my heart and soul.

The kitchen door swings open, and Ivory walks in. She's still dressed in sweats and one of my t-shirts, and she's rubbing her eyes sleepily. When she spots the large quantities of food on the table, she groans.

"What?" Abyss asks, sounding offended.

"Where are the spicy pickles and peanut butter?" Ivory counters as she glares at me. "You know I need those in the morning."

I hurry to the fridge to get the pickles and then to the pantry to get the peanut butter. After setting them both on the table, I smile at her.

"Anything else?" I ask.

"Some chocolate milk and canned tuna."

"Goddamn, woman," Abyss grumbles. "How can you eat that shit?"

Ivory frowns. "Because it's delicious."

My brother shudders. "No, it's not." Pointing to the table, he continues. "Bacon, sausage, eggs, toast, and waffles are deli—"

"Shut up before I puke." She gags and lifts her hand to her mouth as she spins on her heel. "Too late."

She races from the room, and I sigh. "Guess it's gonna be breakfast in bed."

I get a tray from the top of the fridge and load it up with all the weird shit she craves. After adding some bacon and eggs for me, I make my way to my room. The toilet flushes as I enter, and I breathe a sigh of relief that I missed the disgusting stuff.

Don't get me wrong, I'll do anything for Ivory, including holding her hair back and wiping her forehead with a cool washcloth when she's spewing her guts up. But I'm not gonna look a gift horse in the mouth when I'm spared. Fortunately, her bouts of morning sickness are few and far between.

Ivory strolls out of the bathroom, wiping her face on a towel. Her eyes light up when she sees what I'm carrying.

"You're a prince," she says happily.

"I don't know about that," I tease. "Letting you put all this shit in your mouth seems more like a sin than anything."

"And under normal circumstances, I'd agree with

you," she admits, rubbing her belly. "But our son disagrees completely, and he's a demanding little sucker."

Chuckling, I settle on the bed next to her. For the next twenty minutes, I watch her savor each and every bite. I manage to put a little food away, too, but not much because I worry I'll upchuck from the smell of her food pairings.

"That was sooo good," she groans. Ivory licks her fingers clean, moaning at the lingering taste. "Now what?"

I stand and carry the tray to my dresser where I set it down. "Now," I begin, facing her. "You brush your teeth because I wanna kiss the fuck outta you."

Ivory giggles but scurries to the bathroom. I follow, wrap my arms around her from behind, and watch her reflection.

"Maybe we can shower when you're done," I suggest, bobbing my brows.

She spits toothpaste into the sink and rinses her mouth out. "Only if you do that thing."

"What thing?"

"You know... the *thing*." She grins. "With your tongue."

Arching a brow, I smirk. "You mean the thing where I write the ABCs on your nipples with my tongue?"

She leans back against my chest and moans. "Yes, that."

Without responding, I slowly pull her shirt up and over her head. Then I slide her sweats over her hips, letting them pool at her feet. My cock swells when I realize she's not wearing any panties, and I quickly undress before turning the shower on and leading her into the tiled stall.

Warm water cascades over us, but Ivory shivers.

"You cold?"

She shakes her head.

"Horny?"

Nodding frantically, she turns to face me and rests her hands on my chest. "Very."

"We should definitely do something about that."

"Yes, please," she purrs.

I take my time washing her hair and body, letting her pleasure build. It doesn't take much to make her detonate, and I thank my lucky stars for her raging hormones.

As soon as she's clean, I dirty her right back up. The ABCs have never been so erotic. With every pass of my tongue, Ivory moans, and when I lightly pinch her clit, she explodes, her body convulsing.

"That's my girl. Let it all go."

"S-so g-good."

Her knees buckle, and I scoop her into my arms to

carry her to the bed. With her growing belly, missionary is out so she rolls onto her side, and I ease into her from behind.

Our first time together was incredible, but sex has only gotten better with time. Sure, we move slower and with more purpose, but it only adds to the pleasurable sensations.

When my spine begins to tingle, I reach around and roll her clit between my thumb and forefinger. Two more gentle thrusts, and we both come.

We fall back to Earth, and I tug the blanket up over our bodies. "C'mere," I urge, pulling her against my chest.

"I think it's time for a nap," Ivory states, yawning.

"Sleep, sweetheart."

"You'll be here when I wake up?"

I really need to get to work, but Knuckles can handle the shop for the day. Blindly reaching behind me, I snatch my cell off my dresser and send him a quick text. He responds within seconds that he's got things covered, and I kiss the top of Ivory's head.

"I'll be here," I assure her.

"Promise?"

"Promise."

CHAPTER TWENTY-SIX
IVORY

"How's my son doing?"

I squeal as Spike's arms wrap around my stomach. I was so engrossed in my task I didn't even realize he walked in. Turning around in his arms, I stand on my toes to press my mouth against his. I try to step back, but he hauls me closer and deepens the kiss. His tongue demands entry, and I gladly oblige. I moan when Spike's hand cups my ass and his hard cock grinds against me.

"That's fucking hot," Eric groans, and Spike releases me with a grin.

My skin flushes with embarrassment. "What are you doing here, Eric?"

"Megan called and said you might need help loading the van for the trip, but I see you have better things to do."

"Trip?" Spike asks, perplexed.

"Rock climbing excursion and camping after," I explain. "I have to make sure we have everything we need."

"We?"

"Yes, we." I roll my eyes. "Me, Megan, Dale, and Jeremy. We have a lot of climbers. It's my job to make sure we have everything we need. Megan and Dale already safety-checked the equipment so all I have to do is make sure we have all of our supplies."

Spike scowls. "You're not going."

I narrow my eyes. "This is my job, Spike. I'm going."

"You're seven months pregnant, Ivory," he growls. "It's not safe, you're not fucking going. End of story."

I place my hands on my hips. "You will not come in here and dictate what I can or cannot do. I'm a big girl and will do what I damn well please."

He matches my stance. "Over my dead body are you climbing anything."

"No shit, Sherlock," I taunt, waving at my stomach. "Do you honestly think I could get off the ground, let alone climb comfortably? I'm the driver and in charge of setting up the camp. That's it."

"Who's helping you set up the camp?"

I shrug. "No one. The rest of the staff will be dealing with their climbing teams."

"You're setting up tents all by yourself?" Spike asks.

I sigh. "I've done it a million times."

"Not pregnant, you haven't."

Probably not the time to mention I did it a month ago with no issues.

I throw my hands up. "Nothing is going to happen."

"I know because you're not going."

"I. Am. Going." I poke his chest with each word.

Spike opens his mouth to protest more when the sound of a can opening halts our argument.

"Don't mind me," Eric teases. "I needed refreshments to go with the show."

I stomp away from Spike and continue going through my checklist.

"Is she always this fucking stubborn?" Spike complains.

"You have no idea," Eric replies.

"What are the chances I can keep her from going?"

"Unless you're willing to handcuff her to a bed," Eric begins smugly. "My money's on her."

"Hmmm, that's a thought."

"I'm right here!" I shout. "I can hear you."

Spike stalks toward me, but I stand my ground. "I can always take Eric's suggestion. Handcuff you to my bed and fuck you into submission," he murmurs in my ear.

"You can try," I say breathlessly. My mind is already conjuring up images of being at his mercy. I rub my thighs together at the thought.

"You like that, don't ya?" he whispers. "The idea of being at my mercy and coming so hard you see stars?" He bites my earlobe, and I yelp. "Tell me, Ivory. You'd like that a lot, wouldn't you?"

"Yes." I shake my head to clear it of lust-filled thoughts. "But I'm still going on the trip."

"Fine," he replies.

"Fine?"

"Yep, fine. But I'm coming with you."

I cross my arms. "No, you're not."

"I'm either coming with you, or I'm taking Eric's advice."

I shiver. "Okay, but this is my show. You have to listen to what I say *at all times*. We have other people relying on us to get them home safely while providing an amazing experience. This is non-negotiable."

"Deal."

"You can't distract me."

He gathers me in his arms. "Do I distract you, baby?"

"Always," I admit.

"Good." He nibbles on my neck before crashing his mouth down on mine.

My libido fires to life, which has me considering Eric's words. I break the kiss and grin.

"When can we get the handcuffs?"

CHAPTER TWENTY-SEVEN

SPIKE

"You have to secure the corners with th—"

"I know what I'm doing," I snap, glancing at Ivory over my shoulder.

We arrived at the site where we're setting up camp about an hour ago. At first, she tried to do everything, but I quickly shut that down with a jar of spicy pickles and peanut butter. Now, she's happily dictating to me from her seat on a fallen log and snacking.

"Just trying to help," she sasses before dunking another pickle into the peanut butter and taking a large bite.

"How can you eat that shit?" Megan gripes as she drops the last of the supplies on the ground near Ivory. "Just looking at it makes me wanna vomit."

Ivory shrugs. "You'll have to ask our son when he arrives."

Megan shudders. "I'll remember that. I'm gonna

take the climbers to where we'll start our climb and review safety info with them. Need anything from me before I go?"

"Nope," Ivory says and tries to stand. "But I wanna come with you."

"Sit your pregnant ass down," Megan says with a chuckle. "We don't have time to wait for you to waddle over there. It's gonna be dark soon."

My woman pouts but sits back down. "I don't waddle."

The laughter escapes before I can stop it, and she glares at me. "What?" I ask.

"I don't waddle," she repeats.

"Yeah, you do," I insist. "And it's the cutest thing I've ever fucking seen."

"Smart man," Megan teases and walks away.

An hour later, all the tents are set up, and dinner is cooking over a fire. The climbers eagerly talk about tomorrow's adventures while I sit next to Ivory and listen to their excitement.

"I love this," Ivory says absently.

"What?"

She nods at the others in the group. "This. A lot of these climbers have done excursions with us before, but every time it's like it's their first. Nothing beats the adrenaline that comes from what I do for a living, and I love it."

"How long have you been running Chase the High?" I ask, realizing that in all the time we've spent getting to know each other, we never really talked about this.

"Megan and I started it several years back," she says. "I've always been an adrenaline junkie, and she's always supported my habit."

I chuckle. "I get it. That's how it was with Lonnie." Ivory knows the story of how I met Lonnie Jacks and how I became a member of Saints Purgatory. "If not for him, I'd probably be dead or in prison."

"Without Megan, my life would definitely be way less eventful. I'd still be seeking adventure, but I doubt I'd get the same thing out of it if I did it all alone."

"Food's ready," Megan calls out, interrupting our conversation. "Feel free to dig in and stuff yourselves silly."

One by one, climbers and staff fill their paper plates, and we all eat in silence. The meal is a simple one: chili, cornbread, and water. But it's fucking fantastic.

After dinner, two of the guests break out guitars, and we sit around the fire singing and laughing until the moon is high in the sky. Ivory announces that it's time for lights out, and everyone goes their own way into their tents.

"G'night, you two. Try not to be too loud tonight," Megan teases as she zips her tent closed.

Ivory yawns, and I help her to her feet. "C'mon. Let's get some shut eye. You've gotta be exhausted."

She rubs her belly affectionately. "*We* are definitely tired."

I lead her to our two-man tent and ease her to the air mattress I insisted we bring so she can get comfortable. Laying down next to her, I tuck her against my chest, and it's only minutes before a soft snore fills the air. I'm asleep shortly after.

In the morning, light filters through the canvas walls, and I stretch only to realize I'm alone. Scrambling to my feet, I listen for sounds from camp.

"I think I do."

Ivory's voice is the first I'm able to make out, and I smile.

"Might wanna be sure before things go much further," Megan replies.

Are they talking about me?

I duck through the opening, and they both whip their heads in my direction.

"Morning," Megan says.

Ivory walks toward me and rises on her tiptoes to kiss me gently. "Morning sleepyhead," she says when she breaks the kiss.

"You left me again," I accuse, but there's no heat in my words.

She swats me playfully. "Someone's gotta get up and make breakfast. Can't have anyone climbing on an empty stomach."

I want to ask them what they were talking about, but climbers begin to join us, and the moment is gone. Ivory tries to insert herself into every task, and I do my best to stop her from overdoing it. She's not thrilled about it, but she doesn't gripe too much, no doubt not wanting to make a scene in front of the others.

The rock climbing lasts the rest of the day, and I find myself realizing exactly why Ivory loves it so much. I might not be climbing, but it's easy to get caught up in the excitement from the others.

"Wanna head home tonight?" Megan asks when Ivory lies down in the grass just outside of the seating area around the fire.

"Why would we do that?" Ivory asks. "They're all booked through tomorrow."

Megan shrugs. "I just thought... With the pregnancy, I'm sure you'd rather sleep in a real bed."

"I'm fine." Ivory straightens into a sitting position. "I won't let our clients down because I got knocked up."

"No one would be let down," I tell her, unable to

stay out of the conversation. "I'm sure they'd understand."

"No. We're staying, and that's final."

Megan and I exchange a look, but neither of us try to argue.

"Then at least go rest for an hour or so before dinner," I suggest.

"Will that make you both feel better?" Ivory hisses.

"Yes."

"Fine. I'll go *rest*."

I reach down to help her to her feet, but Ivory swats my hand away. Stepping back, I watch her struggle, but eventually, she's upright and waddling away from us.

"Oh, you're so in for a wild ride," Megan taunts.

"Whaddya mean?"

She points at Ivory, who's out of earshot. "That woman is gonna give you a run for your money, biker boy."

I grin. "I'm counting on it."

CHAPTER TWENTY-EIGHT

IVORY

"Are you sure you're ready for this level of commitment?"

Megan watches me with sharp eyes while I tie up some loose ends before going on maternity leave. Spike and I decided the best place for me would be the clubhouse until it was time for Peanut to make his way into the world. Spike feels better knowing that Abyss and Violet can care for me if something were to happen. Turns out Dr. Wilde has a multisite practice and is also registered at Boulder City Memorial. After I heard about that, my mind was made up.

I roll my eyes. "We've been over this," I say for what seems the millionth time. "Abyss is going to be monitoring me until the baby comes. I'll be back after maternity leave, and you can come visit anytime."

Spike and the club gave Megan and Eric access to the clubhouse to visit whenever they want. That was part of our negotiations when Spike approached me about moving in.

"Quit trying to talk her out of moving in with him," Eric scolds, walking into our office like he owns the place. He plops down in his favorite chair. "I, for one, am not missing out on all that yummi-ness, even if I can only look."

Megan smirks. "I'm telling RaRa."

"Heifer!" Eric shouts, no venom in his tone. "Don't you dare! No human being can walk in there and *not* peruse the displays."

"Enough, children." I wince as Peanut kicks my ribs. "That includes you." I tilt my head to my stomach and rub my hands soothingly over my bump.

"That kid is going to be massive," Eric points out. "Be careful he doesn't blow out your hoo-ha."

"Damn it, Eric." Megan cringes. "Keep the commentary to yourself. I don't need those visuals in my head."

We all laugh, and a pang of sadness hits me in the chest. I'm going to miss this.

It's only temporary. You'll be back before you know it.

"Do you want us to come help you pack up?" Eric asks.

"Spike is meeting me in a few hours, but I'm

gonna head out as soon as I finish this paperwork to get a head start."

"You never answered my question," Megan speaks up. "Are you ready for this level of commitment?"

"Little late for that, don't ya think?" Eric mumbles. "She's ready to pop anytime."

We both ignore Eric. Megan walks around my desk, kneels in front of me, and clasps my hands. "Just because you're having his baby doesn't mean you have to jump in with both feet."

I don't even hesitate. "Yes, I'm ready. This is what's best for Peanut."

"Are you absolutely sure this is what's best for you, what you want?" she asks again.

My thoughts are in turmoil as I struggle with answering. Sure, Spike and I have had our ups and downs in our short whirlwind relationship. The fault lies at both of our feet for not communicating. But these last couple of months, we've worked hard to overcome everything that's happened, and not being with him fills me with dread.

"I'm going to be right where I'm meant to be," I state firmly. "I can't imagine not having Spike near me every day. I feel… whole when he's there."

A huge smile spreads across Megan's face. "You love him," she states, conjuring up the conversation we started during the rock-climbing trip… the one Spike interrupted.

Love? Admiration and gratitude because he stepped up, yes, but love?

I let my thoughts wander as the last couple of months with Spike filter through my mind like a projector.

"Omigod!" I whisper. "I love Spike."

Megan stands, pulling me out of my chair, and engulfs me in a hug. "Finally."

I step back, my eyes narrow. "Whaddya mean, 'finally'?"

Megan gestures to Eric. "We've known for a while now," she says smugly. "We were waiting for you to catch up."

How did I not see this? Holy shit… I love Spike.

A tear slips free, and Megan swipes it away. "No tears," she proclaims. "This is a happy day. You're having a baby, moving in with the man you love, and getting a much- needed vacation from this place."

"Very true," I grin. "Too bad you can't say the same."

Megan swats my ass. "You're evil."

I sit back down in my office chair and finish the last of the paperwork. As soon as I'm done, I turn off my computer and grab my cell.

> Me: I'm heading out to start packing

> Spike: Finishing up, be there soon

> Me: Be careful. See ya soon

> Spike: Don't do any heavy lifting

> Me: No promises

Three little dots appear on the screen and then disappear before reappearing again. He knows I won't do anything to jeopardize my health, but I love getting him all riled up.

> Spike: I will tan your ass red. You won't be able to sit for a week

> Me: I'm still waiting on handcuffs. You don't scare me. Unfulfilled promises

> Spike: Baby, don't tempt me, or instead of packing today, I'll spend the day balls deep in your pussy

I squirm in my seat. My panties dampen at the thought of fucking Spike instead of packing.

> Spike: No response, huh?

Me: Guess we'll have to see if you're all talk or a man of action

I drop my cell in my purse, ignoring my pings. Megan's phone goes off. She picks it up and throws her head back, howling.

"You're in so much trouble."

"Not me," I feign innocence.

"Yes, you," she teases. "Spike said to tell you that you better limber up, and he found a pair of handcuffs."

"Kinky." Eric bobs his brows suggestively. "What kind of sex games do you play, Ivory?"

My cheeks flame. "And on that note, I'm outta here." I glance around the office, tears gathering in my eyes. "You'll come to visit?"

Eric embraces me. "Try and stop us."

"I expect daily updates," Megan demands. "Spike better call us when you go into labor."

"He will," I promise.

"Go get your man!" Megan hollers.

I don't need to be told twice. Giving a small wave, I head to my car.

My face hurts from smiling so much as I pull into my driveway. I hum Apple's song *Soul of a Saint* as I unlock my front door and step over the threshold. I drop my purse on the entry table and turn toward the living room where Spike has already taped up several boxes to get me started.

When my eyes land on the person standing several feet away, my legs lock in place for a brief moment due to shock before pure red-hot anger burns through my body.

"Aubrey!" I gasp. "What the hell are you doing here? And how the fuck did you get into my house?"

CHAPTER TWENTY-NINE

SPIKE

"THAT'S ONE LUCKY BABY."

I grin at the saleswoman as she hands me bag after bag of baby items. When I finished up at Sinful Wheels, I decided to stop off at the local baby boutique and spoil my son a bit. Now, I'm running late to meet Ivory at her house, and I'm several thousand dollars poorer.

And so fucking happy I could burst.

Once everything is loaded into the truck, I take my cell out of my cut and hit the speed dial for Ivory. The line rings several times before voicemail picks up.

"Hey, babe," I begin. "I'm running a little late, but I think you're gonna like why. I'll see you soon."

After hanging up, I decide to send her a text as well just to cover my bases.

Me: Running late. Be there soon

Just as I reach the highway, brake lights fill my field of vision. Traffic is backed up for as far as the eye can see. I grab my cell and pull up my traffic app. According to the latest update, there's an accident about ten miles ahead, so I resign myself to being even later to Ivory's.

The hour-long trip turns into two hours. I try Ivory again with no luck, and by the time I turn onto her road, I still haven't received a return call or text from her, but I think nothing of it. She probably has her music turned up while she packs and can't hear it.

Ivory's car is parked in her driveway, and I pull up next to it. I don't bother getting all the bags out of the truck, knowing I'd just have to load them all back up to take to the clubhouse. She'll see everything soon enough.

Music blares from inside the house, and I chuckle at the fact that I was right about why she didn't answer or reply. I yank my keys out of my pocket to unlock the front door but find I don't need them when I turn the knob, and it opens.

"Ivory!" I shout, trying to be heard over the music. "Where ya at, babe?"

My eyes take in the same boxes that were already packed when I left yesterday, and I frown.

Maybe she's taking a bath.

I weave my way through the mess of the living room toward the kitchen to grab a drink before I head to the bathroom. The moment my foot settles on the tile floor, my heart cracks, and my stomach bottoms out.

"Ivory!"

Rushing forward, I take in the sight before me. Ivory is tied to the kitchen table with rope at her wrists and ankles, and she's bleeding heavily. The puddle of crimson on the floor beneath her sends my fear into overdrive.

"Ivory, baby, wake up," I cajole, tapping her cheek and shifting my gaze to her stomach. There's a long jagged incision, and tissue is exposed.

The baby!

I whip out my cell and dial nine-one-one, my mind racing.

"Nine-one-one, what's your emergency?" a female answers.

"I need an ambulance," I snap and rattle off Ivory's address. "She's bleeding heavily, and it looks like…" I swallow the bile creeping up the back of my throat.

"Sir? What does it look like?"

"Fucking hell, it looks like our baby was cut out of her."

I'm not an emotional man, and it usually takes a lot for me to be truly terrified. Right now, I'm both.

"Did you say a baby was cut out of her?" the operator asks.

"Yes!" I shout. "Get a fucking ambulance here!"

Not waiting for a response, I disconnect the call and dial Soul's number.

"Yo, brot—"

"I need you, Abyss, and whoever else you can manage to meet me at the hospital closest to Ivory's address," I spit out.

"What the fuck?" Prez asks. "What's going on?"

"C'mon, Ivory, baby," I plead, squeezing her hand. "Ivory's bleeding out," I tell Soul. "The baby's gone, man." Tears spill onto my cheeks, and I swipe them away before disconnecting the call.

I toss my phone onto the floor and begin CPR. The chances of Ivory living through this are surely next to zero, but I have to do everything I can to save her.

And your son.

Sirens wail in the distance, and I count out my compressions. She has a faint pulse which gives me hope, but I remind myself that life is an evil bitch and likes to kick me in the balls.

Footsteps penetrate the fog of autopilot, and I

glance over my shoulder to see paramedics rushing toward us.

"Sir, I need you to step back so we can work," the older one tells me.

"I'm not leaving her."

"You don't have to leave," he says. "But you do need to give us space."

When I don't move, the younger one forcibly removes me from the kitchen and pushes me into the living room. I watch helplessly as they work to get an IV started.

"Pulse is weak and thready," one of them says. "Based on the amount of blood, I think this is as stable as we're gonna get her here. Let's get a move on and get her to the hospital."

A third paramedic walks by me pushing a stretcher, and the three of them untie Ivory and transfer her from the table.

"You coming?"

I nod absently and follow them outside. I'm dimly aware of locking the front door behind me, but for the most part, all of my focus and attention is on the woman I love, the woman who's dying.

Helluva time to realize how you feel about her.

Climbing into the back of the ambulance, I send up a silent prayer to whatever forces are out there that she'll be okay. I don't know if my prayers are heard, and I'm skeptical that they'll be answered, but I can't sit here and do nothing.

I grab Ivory's hand and brush hair out of her face as the ambulance takes off.

Double dog dare ya to survive.

CHAPTER THIRTY

IVORY

"We can't lose her."

My ears strain to hear Megan's voice, but it's muffled as if my head is underwater. I want to reassure her, but my lips stay sealed together, and my eyelids are dead weight. No matter how hard I fight to open them, they refuse. Everything is numb except for the damn stabbing sensation in my stomach.

My baby!

With renewed strength, I push through the pain. Shoving everything aside, I focus all my energy on my eyes. I groan as I fight the fog.

"She's waking up!" Eric shouts. "Fucking finally."

I blink until the room comes into focus. "Peanut," I mumble.

"It'll be okay, Ivory," Megan reassures, squeezing my hand. "They're out looking."

"Everyone," Eric adds.

"Huh?"

"They'll find him," Eric promises.

Pain assaults me, making it impossible to sit up. My thoughts are jumbled, and I don't understand what they're talking about.

Find who? Spike?

Megan hits the button on the side of the bed to raise my head and adjusts my pillows. Eric lifts a cup and brings a straw to my lips, which I greedily take. I rub my stomach to reassure the baby that we're okay, but my stomach feels hollow under my touch.

"Where's Peanut?" I begin to hyperventilate.

"Breathe, Ivory," Eric encourages. "In through your nose... good, now out through your mouth."

I mimic his breathing until my heart rate slows down.

"What happened?"

"Spike called me when they got you to the hospital," Megan explains as her body shudders. "He found you at the house, unconscious, bleeding out," she says, her voice fading.

"You lost a lot of blood," Eric continues. "They had to do emergency surgery to save you."

The nightmare slams back into me. I was excited to get home to start packing for the big move to the clubhouse.

"Aubrey!" I cry.

"What about her?" Megan asks, swiping hair out of my face.

"Aubrey was in the house," I gush. "She was in my living room, waiting for me. We argued. I don't recall everything, but I *do* remember her standing over me with a knife. Then it goes black again."

Eric puts his cell to his ear. "Yeah… she's awake. Ivory said Aubrey was in the house when she got there… yeah, Aubrey had a knife… okay… bye."

"Who were you talking to?" I inquire.

"Soul," he replies. "They're searching for the baby. They didn't know for sure who attacked you, but they had an idea. You just confirmed their suspicions."

"Spike?"

"Soul's keeping him locked down," Eric says sadly. "He's on a warpath. They can't risk him getting arrested. They're going to find your baby."

"How long have I been here?"

Megan grimaces. "Two days."

That psycho bitch has had Peanut for two fucking days. We'll never find her. What if he's dead? His surgery!

A strangled sob escapes past my lips, and my body convulses involuntarily. Megan gently crawls into the hospital bed with me and wraps me in her arms. She whispers to me that everything will be okay.

My baby is missing. Nothing is going to be okay.

The hospital door opens, startling all of us. I glance over and see a police officer standing right outside.

"What are the police doing here?" I wonder aloud.

A tall gentleman enters my room and approaches my bedside. "Ms. Whitman, I'm Detective O'Malley." I lift my chin in acknowledgment. "I'm sorry I have to do this now when you're trying to recover, but we need your help."

"I don't know how much help I'll be," I admit.

"Do you have any idea who could've done this?"

"Aubrey."

"Who's Aubrey?" Detective O'Malley asks.

Megan takes over. "Aubrey works at Ivory's obstetrician's office. She threatened Ivory a couple of times."

"Why would a random worker threaten you?" He directs the question at me.

"She found out who the baby's father is," I answer.

He checks his notepad. "The father being Hunter Long?"

"Yes," I whisper.

"Was he having an affair with her?"

I shake my head vigorously. "Why are you

standing here asking me questions?" I scream. "My baby is out there somewhere and needs emergency surgery. P-p-please find him."

"We'll find him," he promises.

I see the look in his eye. That look of uncertainty. My heart sinks. Agonizing screams fill the room, but I can't pinpoint where all the noise is coming from.

"Ivory, you have to calm down," Megan pleads.

The screams... They're coming from me. Me! The woman who was cut up and had her baby ripped from her. The person suffering in this bed while her baby is out there somewhere.

A nurse and doctor rush into the room. The nurse holds my flailing arms as the doctor plunges a syringe into my IV.

"This is going to calm you down," he explains. "We can't have you tearing your stitches. You're still at risk for infection."

My screams turn to silent sobs as the medicine seeps into my veins, and my eyelids grow heavy.

"I swear to you, Ivory, Spike will find him," Megan murmurs in my ear.

"Spike..."

His name lingers on my lips as my body shuts down... again.

CHAPTER THIRTY-ONE

SPIKE

"He's gonna hurt himself."

I'm dimly aware of my brothers talking about me as if I'm not here, but I don't give a damn. Lifting another chair, I launch it across the common room. It crashes into the wall and falls to the floor.

"Let him get it all out," Soul says. "He needs this."

Fuck yes, I do. It's been two days, and we're no closer to finding Glitter and my son than we were the second we started searching. The bitch has been a step ahead of us the entire time.

And Peanut is suffering because of it.

Peanut. Peanut. Peanut.

"He doesn't even have a name yet," I say to no one in particular, my shoulders slumping with defeat.

"We're gonna find your boy," Abyss insists, wrapping an arm around my shoulders.

"You don't know that." My breath hitches in my chest. "He needed surgery when he was born, and he didn't get it. He could be dead for all we know."

"Spike, you can't think like that," Soul says, stepping up on my other side. "You've gotta pull yourself together. He needs you, and so does Ivory."

"Oh, God, Ivory." I run my hands through my hair, tugging on it until it hurts. I'd rather feel physical pain than all this emotional agony. "What if she never forgives me?"

"There's nothing to forgive, man." Rogue steps in front of me. "This isn't your fault."

"Yes, it is. I'm the common denominator between Ivory and Glitter. If not for me, she wouldn't be lying in a hospital, recovering from a near-death encounter."

"And neither of you would have found the love of your liv—"

The clubhouse alarm blares, and we all whip our heads in the direction of the elevator. That alarm only sounds when someone who doesn't have access is trying to get into the garage.

"What the fuck?" Malice growls as he strides toward the elevator. He presses the button that opens up a secret door to a monitor. We usually use the security room, but we have this monitor here for emergencies. "Holy shit," he mutters. "You've gotta come look at this."

I rush forward, and when my eyes land on the screen, every muscle in my body tenses.

"Go get her," Soul demands, pointing at Abyss and Rogue.

Glitter is standing directly in front of the camera that covers the outside of the garage, and she's holding a baby. Her eyes appear crazed, and the baby's mouth is open as if he's crying.

"She's got balls showing up here," Soul says. "That's for sure."

"Balls and a death wish," I seethe.

We continue to watch the monitor until Abyss and Rogue appear. Less than a minute later, the elevator door opens, and my living nightmare smiles at me like she isn't on the hook for attempted murder and kidnapping.

"Spike," Glitter says happily. "Come meet our son."

Her cheerfulness shocks me, and I'm at a loss as to what to say or do. Fortunately, Abyss has no such problem.

"Hey, Glitter," he says as he reaches for the baby. "Why don't you let me check him over and make sure he's doing okay while you and Spike talk?"

She wrinkles her nose but nods. "Yeah. Okay."

I breathe a sigh of relief as soon as my son is in Abyss's arms.

"I'm gonna check him out to make sure he's good to make it to the hospital," he says as he rushes toward the medical wing.

I want to follow. Everything in me needs to be with my son right now, but I force my attention on Glitter.

"You fucking bitch," I snarl, grabbing her arm roughly and dragging her across the room. "I'm gonna end your miserable life."

"Spike!" Soul shouts, and I halt. "Let us handle her. You've got more to worry about right now."

"Not on your life," I counter. "She's mine to purge."

"Yeah, great," he says. "You can purge her. But not right this second."

Glitter tries to look at me, but her movements are hampered by my grip. "What's going on, Spike? I thought you'd be happy to see us."

"You're fucking delusional," I spit out.

"But I got rid of that cunt so we could be together," she whines. "We don't have to sneak around anymore. We can be a family."

"What the hell is she babbling about?" Rogue demands.

"Fuck if I know," I reply. "Like I said… delusional."

Glitter rips out of my grasp and straightens to her full height. I'll give her this… she's got no fear.

"I'm not delusional, baby," she says, running her hands up my chest.

I shove her away, and she stumbles. "Touch me again, and it'll be the last thing you ever do."

"But Spike. We're meant to be together. I gave birth to your son. You can't walk away from us."

"You didn't give birth to him. You cut him out of his mother's stomach and stole him." Unable to stop myself, I slap her across the face. "You almost killed Ivory! You could've killed my son!"

Glitter's eyes narrow. "Almost?" She shakes her head. "No. She was dead. I know she was."

"No, she wasn't. I found her just in time," I tell her, enjoying the surprise in her eyes. "She's alive, and so is my son. The three of us are going to be a family. All you're gonna be is fucking dead, you crazy bitch."

"No. No." Glitter presses her hands to her ears as if to block out my words. "It's me and you against the world, Spike. Me, you, and *our* son."

"It's you against Saints Purgatory," Soul snarls. "You against the club and one pissed-off mama."

"Hey, Spike!"

I twist to see Abyss walking toward me with my son in his arms. "Is he okay?"

He places the newborn in my arms and nods. "Yeah. He's underweight and should be in the NICU, and he does need to get to the hospital and have that surgery, but he'll be okay."

Relief washes over me, and I place a kiss on my son's soft head. "Did ya hear that, little man? You're gonna be okay."

"You and Abyss get that boy to the hospital and his mama," Soul instructs. "We'll take care of Glitter."

"I want her alive when I get back," I demand.

"You're not really gonna let them do anything to me?" Glitter shrieks.

Ignoring her, Soul nods. "She'll be breathing."

"Thanks." I turn to walk away, but then a thought occurs to me. "Call the cops and tell them they can call off the search, will ya? Make up some story about how we found him. I don't really care as long as Ivory and I don't have to deal with them."

"Sure thing." Prez smiles. "Go. Put your family back together, Daddy."

"You got it, brother."

"We can't keep calling him Peanut."

Spike and I have been having the same argument for the past couple of weeks. I stroke my fingers over Peanut's arms and legs as he sleeps in the incubator. To keep me from going crazy during the surgery, Spike told me about his childhood and the abuse he suffered. No child should have to endure such trauma. After I threatened to find his parents and kill them with my bare hands, he reminded me about Lonnie Jacks, his mentor and pseudo-father.

Lonnie gave Spike a second chance at life. Now, our son is getting the same second chance.

"Jack," I whisper under my breath, testing it out. It's perfect.

I sneak a peek at Spike, who's staring at our son with adoration. He must sense me staring at him because he lifts me out of the chair and sits down in my place before planting me on his lap. I curl into his chest as we watch *Jack's* little chest rise and fall.

"He's gonna be strong," Spike murmurs in my ear, rubbing my back. "Just like his mama."

"Jack's gonna be a protector like his daddy."

Spike tips up my chin. "What'd you say?"

"I said Jack's gonna be a protector like his daddy."

Spike presses his mouth to mine, gently at first, but it slowly builds into an all-consuming kiss. He stops the kiss before we get kicked out of the NICU.

"Jack, huh?" Spike grins.

"I take it you like the name," I tease.

"Fucking love it."

"I love you," I blurt.

"Ivory," he says, his voice cracking. "I don't deserve you." He presses a finger against my lips to keep me from interrupting. "I'll spend the rest of my life being the best husband to you and father to Jack and however many more kids you're gonna give me. I love you, too."

A tear slides down my cheek, and Spike kisses it away. "Husband, huh?" I cross my arms. "I don't remember you proposing."

Spike smirks. "Don't need to. I'm telling you. It's happening."

"Just like that?"

"Just like that."

Spike lifts me off his lap and stands up. "Let's get some food." Spike tugs my hand, but I hesitate. "You need your strength. You're still healing, too."

Him and his damn logic.

I let him lead me to the cafeteria where we each grab a slice of pizza. After spending almost a month at the hospital, we know which food is edible and what to avoid at all costs. Pizza and salads have become a staple in our diets.

"We haven't talked about it yet," I begin, dropping my voice to a whisper. "What happened to Aubrey?"

The police never found her. According to them, Jack was found on the doorstep of Sinful Wheels, but Aubrey disappeared.

Spike's eyes flash with rage. "She's right where we want her."

"Do I need to worry about her coming after us?" I gulp.

"Never again," he promises. "That cunt will never lay a finger on you or Jack again."

"I believe you," I huff. "I wish I could inflict even half the pain she caused me."

"You'll get your chance," he says cryptically.

"Meaning?"

"I had to force myself through perdition, thinking

I lost you both and how I'd live without you," he explains. "That bitch never stood a chance from the moment she put her hands on you. Add in the fact that she took our boy, she's lucky the old ladies haven't already killed her." He pauses, his gaze leveled on mine. "Glitter is at the club, chained to a wall, awaiting her fate."

"Good."

"Good?" Spike arches a brow. "You're okay with this?"

I nod. "Absofuckinglutely"

He pulls me close. "How long until I can fuck you senseless?"

"Three more weeks," I pout.

Spike winks. "It's a date."

We throw away our garbage and head back to the NICU. The pediatrician is performing her exam when we enter.

"Oh, good," she exclaims. "Just the parents I wanted to see."

"Dr. Roberts," Spike greets. "We gettin' good news today?"

"Actually, you are," she confirms. "We're going to remove the feeding tube tonight and start bottle feeds."

I grip Spike's hand tightly. "Are you serious?"

"Yes, you're just in time."

The staff is gentle as they remove his feeding tube. Jack squirms and lets out a disgruntled cry.

"Can I breastfeed?" I've been pumping my milk so it wouldn't dry up because I want to be able to breastfeed Jack.

"Not yet, but soon," she states. "If you have breast milk stored, you can feed that to him from a bottle. We need to document how much he's able to eat and if he has any issues with swallowing."

"I've been pumping," I announce proudly.

"Great." Dr. Roberts signals to a nurse. "Can we get Ivory a bottle for her breast milk and set her up to do Jack's first feeding?"

The next twenty minutes, I'm an emotional wreck as I hold Jack and feed him his first bottle. I cry and then burst into giggles. He takes the bottle beautifully without any issue. Once he's finished, I hand him to Spike, and my heart melts.

Spike cradles Jack to his chest. "That's my big boy."

Two days later, we have our discharge papers. Spike carefully buckles the car seat in and lifts me into the SUV, securing me as well.

"You know, I've been strapping myself into cars since I was kid," I admonish.

"You're precious cargo." Spike places a quick kiss on my lips. "I'm not taking any chances."

"Okay," I say breathlessly.

Spike climbs into the driver's seat and starts the engine. "Ready to go home?"

I grin. "Let's go!"

Not only am I ready to go home, I'm ready to end that miserable bitch.

CHAPTER THIRTY-THREE

SPIKE

"WELCOME HOME!"

I grin as Ivory and I step off the elevator and are greeted by shouts of excitement from my family.

Our family.

"I wanna see Jack," Skye announces, walking in our direction. She has her arms extended and is making cooing noises. "Gimme that baby."

Ivory hands her the carrier gently, careful not to wake Jack. He slept the entire way home from the hospital, and if I remember correctly from when Harper, Soul and Cece's daughter, was an infant, sleep doesn't always come so easily.

"We're so glad you're home," Soul says, slapping me on the back. "And we're thrilled to have you here, too," he tells Ivory.

"Thanks. There's nowhere else I'd rather be," she replies. Then her gaze wanders as if she's looking for someone. "Where is she?"

No clarification is needed. "She's in the Confessional," I tell her. "Why don't you and Jack get sett—"

"Take me to her," Ivory demands.

"Are you sure?" Soul asks. "Nothing has to be done right away."

"I need to know that that bitch is dead before I touch my son again. I need to know that she can't taint our lives with her evilness." She takes a deep breath. "So… Take me to her. Now."

Soul and I exchange a look, and then I lead her across the room and onto the second elevator that only goes down.

"This isn't gonna be pretty," I warn.

"Not looking for pretty, Spike. I'm looking for complete obliteration."

When we step into the hallway just outside the Confessional, I link my fingers through hers and force her to face me.

"Ivory, once you take a person's life, there's no going back. That's not something that can be undone, so I need you to be sure this is what you want. Because if you're not, I can handle it on my own."

She takes a deep breath, rage entering her brown eyes. "I've never been more sure of anything in my life."

"Anything?" I tease, tilting her chin up.

"Anything other than loving you and Jack," she clarifies sweetly.

"Okay, then. Let's do this."

Ivory hesitates for a moment when the door to the Confessional opens, but she quickly squares her shoulders and strides inside. I follow.

"Oh, Spike, I'm glad you're home."

I see Glitter's still delusional.

"What's wrong, bitch?" Ivory snaps. "You sound a little weak."

Glitter is hanging from chains connected to the ceiling. The tips of her toes barely touch the floor, and she's emaciated. My brothers did a great job keeping her just at the brink between life and death.

"Who're you?" Glitter asks, glaring at Ivory.

I can't tell if she really doesn't know or if she's faking it, but I'll play her game if she wants. Unfortunately, Ivory doesn't give me the chance to play.

"I'm the woman you tried to kill. Remember cutting open my stomach, pulling my baby from my belly, and leaving me to die tied to my kitchen table? Do you really envy me that much?"

Glitter's eyes light up. "Oh, yeah. I seem to recall something like that. And I wouldn't call how I feel about you *envy*. It's more like an intense hatred because you tried to take what's mine."

Close enough.

"Did Spike give you the good news?" Ivory asks as she stalks toward the wall of weapons.

"Good news?"

Ivory lifts a serrated knife from the hooks it rests on and turns back toward Glitter. "Yeah. The news that Jack survived."

"Jack?"

"Our son," I clarify.

"My baby lived?" she counters.

Ivory snaps, lunging forward and thrusting the knife into Glitter's side. "He's not your son," she snarls.

Glitter howls in pain, and her eyes flutter as she fights unconsciousness. "I-is that a-all ya got?"

"Don't tempt her," I warn.

"Just kill me, and get it over with," Glitter says, her voice barely loud enough to hear.

"Oh, don't you worry," Ivory says, flipping the knife over in her hand. "You're gonna die. But first, you're gonna suffer."

"Do I get a turn?" I ask hopefully before she can deliver another stab.

Ivory shrugs. "Sure."

I grab one of several railroad spikes off the wall, grinning with anticipation. When I turn back around to face Glitter, satisfaction rolls through me at her look of fear.

Finally, she gets it.

"Damn." Ivory whistles. "And here I thought the knife was bad."

Waving the spike in front of my face, I take in the rust covering the surface. "I find that old and dull works best for maximum pain."

Without warning, I take two strides forward and jab the spike into Glitter's thigh. Her mouth drops open, but no scream erupts as she passes out.

"Well, shit," Ivory grumbles. "I wanted to do more."

"She's not dead, babe," I assure her. "You can still have some fun."

"Oh, goody." Her tone gives way to the giddiness she's feeling. "Any suggestions?"

"Try to avoid major arteries if you want her alive longer."

"Right."

Ivory walks in circles around a dangling Glitter for several long minutes. And then... BAM!

She delivers stab after stab after stab. Blood pours from each and every wound, slowly draining Glitter of her life force. I lose track of how many injuries Ivory inflicts, but that doesn't stop the pride from welling inside of me.

She's the one. No doubt about it.

Eventually, Ivory tires out and stumbles into my chest.

"I'm done," she announces, her voice drowsy. "You finish her off."

"With pleasure."

I don't let go of Ivory as I grip the spike in my hand and thrust it into Glitter's jugular. A few minutes later, the bleeding stops.

"Go forth, sinners' souls, from this world. May you suffer in darkness, may your home be in Hell, and may the Devil fuck you with his horns."

Ivory tips her head up to look at me. "What was that?"

"Just something we say when we purge something."

"Can I say it?"

"Absolutely."

I begin again, and Ivory repeats my words.

"...Devil fuck you with his horns."

"I love you," I say, spinning her around so I can lift her into my arms.

Ivory wraps her legs around my waist and kisses me passionately.

"I love you, too," she says once the kiss ends. "Now, take me upstairs so I can shower and feed Jack."

"Yes, ma'am."

"Oooh, I think I like the sound of that."

"I'll keep that in mind."

EPILOGUE

IVORY

Three months later . . .

"M<small>EGAN</small> <small>GOOD WITH YOU STEPPING BACK</small>?" S<small>PIKE</small> <small>ASKS</small> as he peels back the comforter and slips in beside me.

"More than okay," I assure him. "Jeremy's practically been running things with her since I've been gone. He's excited for the promotion."

After my near-death and Jack's kidnapping, I did some soul-searching. I can't justify taking such risks with my life anymore. I have a family to think about, and it's not fair to them to worry about me every time I leave for the day or an extended trip. Spike agreed but never pressured me. I'll still be a co-owner of *Chase the High* and help when I can. But there'll be no more dangerous activities.

"Good." Spike nibbles on my neck and palms my breast.

I melt into his touch and groan. His hand dips lower, caressing my body as he teases my belly button. His fingers skim the outline of my panties before his hand pushes under the waistband. Spike rubs my clit fast, applying the right amount of pressure to make me come undone.

His mouth covers mine to silence me as I scream my release. The last thing either of us want to do is wake up Jack. He's finally thriving, but it took us a couple of weeks to get his schedule fixed. Our little boy decided he'd rather be up at night and sleep during the day. We're finally on a normal sleep schedule, and there's no way we're going to wreck that.

I grip Spike's cock, but he gently pulls my hand away. He kisses me gently before rolling me over and pressing his front to my back, wrapping his arms around me.

"Tonight is about you," he whispers.

"Love you." I snuggle into his warmth.

"Love you."

Spike and I sleep soundly, and the last thing I expect when I wake up is to be ushered off to a tattoo parlor. Yet, that's exactly where I am… and breast-feeding Jack, no less.

When I pictured my bachelorette party, I imagined drunkenness and strippers, not this. However, this is much better.

"What color did you decide on?" Skye asks.

"Pink," I reply. "Not very badass, I know."

"The color doesn't mean shit." Jez plops down next to Skye. "The person wearing the tattoo is a badass, and girl you *are* a complete badass."

I shake my head, but Violet speaks up. "You survived. That takes more courage than letting death take you."

"Hell, yeah!" Cece cheers.

"As President of the Badass Bitches Club, I feel I should say a few words," Carmella chimes in.

"This ought to be good," Cece mumbles.

"Can it, Hooker." Carmella narrows her eyes. "As I was saying… We gather here today to welcome the newest member to the BBC."

Megan spits out her drink. "BBC?" she chokes.

Carmella groans. "I know, I hear it now."

Everyone bursts out laughing.

"To Ivory," Apple shouts.

"Oh, no. This is all your fault." I glare at Apple.

Apple sits back shocked. "What did I do?"

"You're the reason I got knocked up," I accuse.

"Um…" Megan speaks up. "Pretty sure that was Spike's fault."

I shake my head. "Nope, this is all on Apple. I would've just danced with him and let it go, but oh, no, she had to go and sing *Soul of a Saint*."

"Oh, yeah," Cece agrees. "Totally Apple's fault. That song makes every woman within a two-mile radius horny."

"It should come with a damn warning label," I joke.

"Noted." Apple smiles. "But you got one helluva a little man out of it."

"And a big one," Violet adds.

"Alright," I concede. "You're forgiven."

I switch boobs and notice the room has gone quiet. "What's wrong?"

Apple giggles. "I think you broke Possum."

Possum is staring at Jack with a look of wonder on his face. "Oh, fuck. Sorry, Ivory," he apologizes.

"Better hope Spike doesn't kick your ass for staring at his woman's tits," Carmella teases.

"Shit," Possum mutters.

"I won't tell," I whisper.

"I will," Jez promises.

Possum grimaces. "Can you at least wait until after the wedding, so I don't have a black eye?"

"Sure," Jez says cheerfully. "It'll be my wedding gift to Spike."

"Where are you going to get it?" Megan asks, taking Jack from me. "The tattoo, I mean."

"On my shoulder," I reply.

Possum fires up the tattoo gun. Surprisingly, all I feel is peace. Never in a million years did I think I'd ever get something permanently inked on my body. After having Jack literally cut out of me, though, needles aren't as scary anymore.

Violet's right. I survived. We survived.

Spike

One week later…

"You ready, brother?"

I glance at my reflection in the mirror in the gym. When I asked Ivory to marry me, I was fully expecting her to want me in a monkey suit for the ceremony, but she surprised me when she said that she wanted everything to be more casual.

"More than ready," I reply to Thorn.

He's helping me get ready while the rest of the brothers set up the common room and the old ladies help Ivory with Jack.

"I can't believe she said yes."

"Dude, she had my kid," I remind him. "Of course, she said yes."

"It all makes sense now," he taunts. "She felt obligated."

"Shut the fuck up."

Thorn laughs. If it weren't for the small matter of a wedding ceremony, I'd beat the shit out of him.

Before we can continue our banter, Mark walks into the gym. "Everything's ready."

I nod at him, silently wondering when we're gonna vote on the prospect's patch. When we were all so busy with Ivory and finding Jack, he really stepped up to handle Carter Maxwell's purge. Normally, we wouldn't want a prospect involved too much in that, but it couldn't be helped.

Besides, he's Malice's brother and has earned the right to show us what he's made of.

"Let's get this show on the road," Thorn announces several minutes later, breaking into my thoughts. "Keep her waiting too long, and she's liable to walk right out of the clubhouse."

Shaking my head, I roll my eyes and follow him out of the gym. The common room looks amazing, and my heart stutters in my chest as I take my place at the makeshift altar.

The music starts, and Apple begins to sing *Soul of*

a Saint. I can't stop the laugh that barrels out of my chest. Ivory must've arranged this because I don't remember planning it.

My vision blurs when Ivory steps into sight. She's wearing a strapless, floor-length dress and has never looked more beautiful. When she reaches me, she twists, showing me the tattoo on her shoulder that she's managed to keep hidden since she got it.

"I love it," I whisper.

"I love you," she says.

The ceremony goes by without a hitch. Jack, bless his tiny heart, is quiet through the whole thing, waiting until I'm told to kiss the bride to start wailing.

Ivory groans but with a smile. "Guess he's hungry."

I pull her close. "So am I."

My old lady winks. "Meet me in our room in thirty."

"You got it."

Ivory takes Jack from Cece while I address everyone.

"Sorry, guys, but duty calls. Feel free to kick off the party, and we'll join you as soon as we can."

Cheers and good-natured ribbing fills the room, as well as my soul. This is the life I was destined for, the family I deserved all along.

I join Ivory and Jack in our room. Ivory's eyes are closed, but she's not sleeping, and Jack's tiny fist kneads her breast as he sucks.

Ivory and Jack. Jack and Ivory.

The only two people in the universe who make me feel whole.

IF YOU HAVEN'T READ THE OTHER BOOKS...

If you haven't read the other books in the Saints Purgatory MC series:

Start with book 1: Unholy Soul

There isn't a person in the world who hasn't committed a sin. Some sins are worse than others, but seven of them are deadly. But those seven worst of the worst? They're what drive Saints Purgatory MC to keep fighting.

SOUL

What is a person supposed to do when they learn the world is a breeding ground for evil? As the president of Saints Purgatory MC, it's my job to lead my brothers in the war against the wicked. Not only do we find transgressors in our day-to-day lives, but my twin sister regularly brings us the names of sinners.

In my world, love doesn't exist. At least not the healthy kind. But when we're charged with eliminating a doctor with a tendency for sloth, everything changes. His patient barrels her way into my life and my heart, and I will stop at nothing to ensure she's mine. Even if that means letting her see the darkest parts of my soul.

It's not lost on me that to do what we do, we must become the very thing we despise. Hell, it's our club motto: *See evil, hear evil, become evil, purge evil.*

CECE

I love my life. I'm a business owner, a daughter, and a friend. But two words are all it takes to send me spiraling into chaos. Obstacles are continually hurled at me from every direction. My world is ripped apart and it takes everything I have not to lose my mind.

After the latest middle finger life flips me, fate steps in and offers me a lifeline. Too bad it's in the form of a dominating, possessive, *sexy as sin* man. I've always considered myself to be independent, but just this once, I want to give in and let him take care of me.

Retribution is the man's promise, but can he deliver? Can I trust a stranger to help me, when there's more at stake than revenge? Or will my heart suffer the consequences?

Welcome to Saints Purgatory, where sinners take out the sinful.

ALSO BY

ANDI RHODES & LACY ROSE

Saints Purgatory MC

Unholy Soul

Wrathful Malice

Grim's Hell

Shadowy Abyss

Rogue's Cross

Thorned Vengeance

Spike's Perdition

ABOUT THE AUTHORS

Andi Rhodes is an author whose passion is creating romance from chaos in all her books! She writes MC (motorcycle club) romance with a generous helping of suspense and doesn't shy away from the more difficult topics. Her books can be triggering for some so consider yourself warned. Andi also ensures each book ends with the couple getting their HEA! Most importantly, Andi is living her real-life HEA with her husband and their boxers.

For access to release info, updates, and exclusive content, be sure to sign up for Andi's newsletter at andirhodes.com.

Lacy Rose is an author who loves to write gritty MC (motorcycle club) romance. Lacy loves multiple genres and can be found reading almost anything in her free time. She lives with her husband of 23 years and two children. When she isn't writing, her life is often filled with mayhem from kids' school activities, so she reads and writes in her free time to escape reality. Lacy enjoys sharing her stories with others, and they always have a HEA.